Beyond Repair

Part 1

Damaged Duet

Y.V. Larson

Trigger Warning

Please read the following list if you have any triggers. Note that these could be considered spoilers!

If you have any questions, you may reach out to me through social media, or via email: Author@yvlarson.com

- Kidnapping
- Psychiatric facility (mentioned)
- Nightmares
- PTSD responses
- Flashbacks
- Scars
- Dog bite (mentioned) (scarring)
- Fear of dogs
- Torture (mentioned)
- Eating disorder (FMC struggles with a small appetite)
- Suicidal ideation
- Aversion to touch

Trigger Warning

- Anxiety
- Mental health struggles

For those who feel broken.

Prologue

Nina

2.5 years ago

Fire radiates from every beaten inch of my body. The slice of tree branches assaulting my bare arms, face, and legs is nothing compared to the sheer agony nipping at the back of my calves.

A delirious little snort tumbles from my bloody lips as my feet tumble to get me away.

Nip...

The punch line is that I literally got nipped by his dog as I made my escape. V*iciously* bitten, actually. If body parts could scream, the steady stream of blood running from my right calf would help me pass as a banshee staggering through these godforsaken woods.

So many trees...many, many...many trees.

On and on it goes. My frantic hunt for freedom, for help, never seems to come. *So many trees.*

A rattle shakes my vocal cords as green and brown whip by me and waver in the setting sun. Another wheeze burns my

1

lungs, this one threatening my impending doom. Suffocating darkness steals my peripheral vision like a demon damning me to eternal misery. Soon, I won't be able to see anything, whether in death or nightfall.

At the time, escaping in broad daylight made sense because there was an obvious opening. Now, though, I swear my sickly pale skin and long hair flash like a beacon in the gold streaks taunting me from above.

"Please," I whisper, only for my plea to dissolve into a pained cry when my ankle twists. The sharp ache is immediately accompanied by a throb in my shoulder as I careen into a tree.

"Ouch!" I hiss, collapsing against the rough bark. Tears scorch my heated cheeks while sweat burns every single scrape dotting my dirty flesh. "Come on...come on, Nina."

I can barely make out my whimpers, but still I suck in a deep breath and *feel* every single desire and absolute *need* to keep running. *I have to keep running.*

Light flashes ahead of me, streaking through the trees. Then another. And another brighter than the last, as the sun leaves me on this rotten planet to find my own way in the darkness. Another flash, and this time I hear a *whoosh* as it goes. *Run. RUN! RUN!*

"Ahh!" It's a battle cry and terrified shout all in one as I push away from the tree I've bloodied, then pump my frail legs as hard as I can, all the while terrified they will snap at any moment.

Another flash. "Oh my g-god," I sputter and trip in my distracted haste to get to what I think is a road. My arms flail, my left leg shoots forward faster than planned and catches me before I fall, only for the ground to drop out from beneath me.

I can't even scream as I tumble hands-first into a deep ditch that may as well be my final resting place for all the fight I have left in me.

Climb! The voice sounds familiar. Soft and throaty, enough to make me want to melt into a puddle.

CLIMB! This one is more frantic and energized, buzzing my insides enough for my chin to lift out of the dirt.

CLIMB, NINA! Stark fear and accusation whip through my mind, delirium making me think Ridge is standing above me and aggressively begging me to move.

FUCKING CLIMB! At the harsh demand of the final voice, I groan and begin to crawl.

One agonizing handful of grass after another, I finally scrape my nails on asphalt. All I can think as light blinds me and screeching tires deafen me, is *I'm so grateful to have felt them one last time, even if it was a hallucination.*

Chapter 1

Nina

"*It's time, sweet Nina.*"

Dad didn't mean it in the way I took those words. I *knew* he wasn't suggesting I just move on. No, he just meant I should move out. *Live.*

How could he possibly think I would ever be ready to leave?

"*I agree with your dad, sweetheart.*"

If dad's statement stunned me, my mom's had thrown me headfirst into a sobbing mess. Loneliness crept in on my heart that day, even as my mom cried along with me. Their embrace of love and support only served to remind me that soon I wouldn't have this.

They didn't say those things to make me feel bad, but to encourage me to start living my life again. Because an almost twenty-one-year-old should *want* to move out and live an independent life. And who would ever turn down full financial support and a small house on their parents' dime?

Me. I tried to say no. I tried *really* dang hard. I *begged.*

"*I'm not ready,*" I wept, hoping they would see the terror

ripping me apart. Two and a half years wasn't enough; how did they not see that?! My parents gave me sad smiles, and I knew they had made the decision for me.

Ready or not, I had to figure out how to survive on my own in one month and two days.

" **N**ina!"
My eye twitches in vague awareness of Mom's shout, yet her call coasts over me like a puff of air.

Absently, I tug on the strings of my fluffy beige pillow. The dry texture between my fingers keeps me here in the present. A time and place I don't want to be but subconsciously know is my only option. Because if I drift far enough away, I worry I'll fall right back into that basement. The basement that sucks me in and torments me every night. It's been two and a half years since I escaped, but I brought plenty of that hell home with me.

I'll never truly be free.

Even if the monster is ever caught and sentenced to life behind bars, or killed, I'll still never be free. The things he did to me will always stain my soul and scar my mind.

I can't think without stumbling over another wound that healed in a jagged, puckered tripwire that slams the alarm on all my trauma responses.

Trauma responses. That's what all my therapists have called my issues. How can they put a label on all the darkness sucking the life out of me?

I'll never be free. No matter what I'm labeled, I'm still stuck in that basement, being starved and beaten.

Phantom pains is what my doctors call the lingering aches

in my knees from scrubbing the monster's floor until I collapsed.

"NINA!"

The pillow tumbles off my lap with the wicked force of my fearful jump. My shaky hand clasps at my chest, begging my heart to calm down.

"Y-yes?"

The door handle rattles, and there's murmuring on the other side of the door. "Unlock the door." *Shoot, I hate when Dad's mad.*

Cringing, I scoot to the edge of my bed and leave its comforting warmth. Chills race up my calves from the hardwood floors under my bare feet. It may be summer in Utah, but I won't ever get my bones to unfreeze from the basement that sucked the heat right out of me.

I can't help but curl in on myself as I unlock and twist the handle. *They're mad.* Cracking the door open reveals my parents' frantic gazes that search for any signs of injury.

I've never harmed myself. At least not on purpose. I may forget to eat and hydrate myself. Sometimes I'll sleep for eighteen hours or only close my eyes for forty minutes a night, but I've never sought to inflict pain.

After all these years, I have no idea how to convince myself I'm not in that hellhole anymore. It's as if I still function like I did when I was in captivity for eighteen months.

"Yes?" I whisper, stepping back and away from my dad's towering height. He would never hurt me, and I yearn for him to wrap me in his arms, but I know I've disappointed him by locking the door.

"You know what happens when you don't listen..."

I gulp and shudder, my body actively trying to push the monster's voice from my mind.

Dad's eyes soften a fraction as he studies me. "Nina, why

did you lock the door?" I shrug, not remembering actually doing it. He sighs. "We talked about this."

You did, I want to say. Coming home after a year in a psych facility, my parents were scared, and rightfully so. They were worried I would do something like kill myself, I think. So the door to my bedroom was removed, and my bathroom door didn't have a lock. Until a few months ago. Apparently, they're still afraid of what I might do if I'm alone.

"I—" I hesitate, not sure if I should speak my mind. I never complained about the lack of privacy or asked for my door back. It didn't matter, not much does except my parents and our home. It was an unconscious decision to lock the door. Maybe it was to help me feel safe.

"What, sweetheart?" Mom encourages, her eyes imploring me to finish my thought.

"I guess I didn't realize that was still a thing. Since, you know..." I pick at the string hanging from my long T-shirt. "I'm moving out."

Mom deflates and immediately looks at dad like he can fix this. Fix *me*. Once again, my dad sighs and scrubs a hand through his dark greying hair.

"You're right. We were just..."

When he trails off, I only nod. What is there to say? I know I'm not normal, heck I barely look alive, so why would they think I *wish* to be alive?

Do I want to be alive? I have no clue how to answer that now, just like I didn't know how to answer it at the psych facility. I'm positive nobody believed my answers when they were doing the suicide screening before I could be discharged.

I'm not sure what it feels like to be alive anymore, so how would I know? I barely have the energy to sit through an entire movie, let alone end my life.

"We found a house," Mom says cheerfully, if not a little hesitant.

My heart sinks to my belly and I have to fight to keep the tears from building in my eyes.

"And it's all yours, sweet Nina," Dad adds with a big smile. There's sadness in his gaze too.

I can't smile back, because even if I'd rather not die, I don't want to live either. A house of my own...I'm about to be forced to do exactly what I'm afraid of.

I'm scared to live.

Chapter 2

Nina

"It's almost an hour away!" Dad's answering glare does nothing to tamp down my panic. "No, I'm not moving that far away from you guys."

"Nina. I don't want to tell you that you're being dramatic, but thirty-seven minutes is not an hour," Dad explains as he tries to hold on to his patience. "It's the perfect gap between us. Provo will be good for you. It's a college town. You'll have people your own age."

"Maybe even people you knew back then!" Mom's cheerful, but the blush on her cheeks tells me there is more to this plan that I'm not being told.

Saliva fills my mouth. "I don't want to see anyone from before." *Before I was kidnapped...*

We've gone over this so many times since I moved back home. My parents think it would be good for me to see my childhood friends, but I can't fathom how that would go. I'm nowhere near the same person they used to know. Plus most of my close friends were guys. My dad makes me wary enough and I love him like he's my other half.

Mom's frowning from across the table like she can't figure me out. "You risk seeing someone from before every day if you stay in Herber."

"It's not like I leave, or want to leave anyway," I grumble, wanting to bash my head on the laptop keys shoved in front of me.

Arguing makes me want to throw up, but the shock of how far they're moving me away has loosened my tongue. I haven't thought about the repercussions of my actions, but the longer my mom and dad stare at me in baffled silence, the more my anxiety rises.

"It's a pretty house..." I concede quietly, hoping to alleviate the tension. And it *is* nice.

A four bedroom, two bath brick home in a quiet neighborhood was more than I would have expected my parents to buy me. The inside photos make the house seem warm and cozy with an air of isolation that will serve as my perfect safe space.

"We thought it was perfect," Mom says softly, like she's worried about my opinion. "Enough bedrooms for us to spend the night, and maybe an office for yourself for if you decide to go to school."

And there it is. "I'm not going to BYU, Mom."

"Why not? It was your dream school, sweetheart. I'm not saying you have to go right away, but being close by will be the perfect opportunity to follow your dream."

Mom's defense sparks an unknown feeling in me. One that makes my belly and chest ache with longing and despair. "It wasn't my dream to go alone," I whisper, struggling to keep my tears in check.

Mom shares a look with Dad and I know it has everything to do with me. "I know you miss them."

"I don't," I murmur, hunching over the screen in faux interest in my new house.

Dad's hand yanks the laptop away from me. "Knock it off. Nina, you're not fifteen anymore. You know denial doesn't make the hurt go away. You're almost twenty-one. Speak to your mother like an adult."

"Will..." Mom whispers, touching my dad's hand cautiously. She knows what's going to happen next.

I've worn out the space allotted for my opinions. I'm exhausted and just plain tired. Arguing, speaking my mind, being an adult or even childish takes so much out of me. I wasn't allowed to be anything except a bloodied servant for eighteen months, and sometimes I miss the clear rules the monster set out for me.

Don't speak.

Don't scream.

Don't cough.

Don't sneeze.

Don't scuff your feet.

Don't stomp.

Don't fight back.

Don't roll your eyes.

Don't think.

Don't feel.

Don't exist beyond duty.

"*Just do as you're told. Don't give me any reason to teach you what happens when you break the rules.*"

"Okay."

My bland response is met with a choked sigh from my mom and my dad's head drooping low. Whether I open my mouth or stay invisible, I'm always upsetting them. I love my parents so much that if moving out is what they need to be happy again, I'll do it.

"Thank you," I add, scooching my chair back silently, and leaving the kitchen without a sound.

And I *am* thankful.

Chapter 3

Ridge

No amount of zombies can take my mind off the one thing that is sure to make me crumble.

I pride myself on being a pretty decent, outgoing, fun guy, but sometimes I'm none of those things. When I can't get her out of my head, I become a shell of myself. Broody is what Kai likes to call it.

Pop, pop, pop!

Guts spatter the ship deck on the TV screen, but I feel no better than I did when I drew the damn portrait that's taunting me.

"You could move it, Ridge."

Scowling, I try to ignore Kai's soft words. Damn him for being so intuitive and fuck me for being transparent.

"Dude..."

"What, Kai?" I snap, not daring to look at him.

He sighs and I see him stand from the dining room table. I try to pay him no mind, but I can't control the way my body stiffens when he grabs the sketchbook. "Beautiful," he murmurs, sitting beside me.

I grunt, partly because there's nothing to say and to clear the lump from my throat. *Of course she's beautiful.*

It's silent for a few minutes, and for that I'm grateful. Of course it doesn't last long. "You gotta stop torturing yourself, man. This is happening more and more lately."

My first mistake is glancing at him, the second is getting sucked into the obvious longing twisting his features, and the third is getting eaten by a zombie. *There went my distraction.*

Frustrated, I toss the controller down on the cushion beside me and scrub my hands down my face. "I can't help it," I grumble and tug the portrait out of his hands. He's reluctant to let it go, *let her go,* but he relents and studies the charcoal lines I drew over my shoulder.

Kai clears his throat subtly, but not enough to hide the emotion that's clogging his words. "That's one of your best."

I nod, but we both know I'll never be able to recreate the sheer beauty that was our Nina. "I can't stop picturing her, Kai. No matter how many times I put her on paper, she doesn't go away. She's haunting me."

As I whisper my sorrows, I take in Nina's beach waves and her glorious eyebrows. Nothing I draw does her justice. The placement of her spattering of freckles will never be accurate, nor will her smile shine on the page like it did in real life.

I don't add color to these portraits, knowing I won't get her brown hair right or capture the full depth in Nina's grey-blue eyes.

"Nina's *not* haunting you, Ridge. She wouldn't do that even if she were—"

Dead, Kai was going to say. It's been almost five years. If she is alive, it breaks my heart to worry if death would be a mercy for my sweet girl.

Nina was full of spice and fire, always running around and wild. Everybody wanted to be her friend, and she made it so.

Her kindness knew no bounds unless you put a mitt or bat in her hands. That girl was competitive as fuck with any sport or game. Softball, though? That made her competitiveness take on a whole other level.

"God, she used to whoop our asses on the field."

Kai snorts and leans back. "Yeah she did. Scared the shit out of me every time she asked to play a game."

My right hip tingles as we talk about Nina with a baseball bat. One of the first times we ever played a game, she hit a line drive straight into my fucking hip bone. I fell in love right then and there.

"But lord help you if you said no," I add, smiling softly at my girl. It kills me that she's been reduced to memories.

"You know I can't say no for shit." Kai huffs and I finally take a good look at him. His beard is trimmed short, but it's longer than scruff these days. An easy, wistful smile tilts his lips. "You shoulda heard the damn coffee order I had to ask the poor barista to make Henry this morning. I was so embarrassed."

I laugh loudly this time. "You're wrapped around his finger."

"Always have been," Kai agrees with a smirk.

"Always will be!" Henry hoots, appearing out of nowhere and snuggling into Kai's side. "What's up? Oh."

And just like that, Henry's spurt of energy dissolves when he sees my sketchbook on my lap. Sighing, I place it on the coffee table in front of us. Fucking hell, I hate when Henry retreats. Where I turn into a broody asshole, Henry gets sad and quiet. It sets all of us on edge. He's our sensitive soul, and I just ruined his mood for the foreseeable future.

Kai drops a kiss on his partner's unruly black curls. "Just reminiscing," Kai explains, but we've already lost Henry to his thoughts.

Trevor glides into the room, brows furrowed, immediately

picking up on the melancholy vibes. My cousin's permascowl softens when he sees my latest sketch. His wide shoulders slump, making my stomach cramp with guilt. *Maybe I should start hiding my shit.*

"Can I have that one?" Trev murmurs, dropping into one of our recliners.

"Of course." Sometimes they ask to keep them, Trevor more than Henry and Kai. We lapse into silence and instead of breaking it, I toss my cousin a controller, then start up another game of Zombies.

We miss you, Nina.

Chapter 4

Nina

My bedroom is decorated in soft purples and grays. I love my bedspread the most with its swirly flowers and heavy feel.

Four boxes of clothes surround me on the floor, and I know I need to figure out what else I'm going to pack, but that's the problem. What am I supposed to bring?

This has always been my childhood bedroom and I have never once changed it. I remember coming home for the first time since I was sixteen after...well, everything horrible, and being shocked to see my parents hadn't changed a thing.

It's been my safe space ever since. If I'm being honest with myself, it's becoming harder to live here. As upset as I am about my parents encouraging—*forcing*—me to move out—*move on*—there's a sense of relief in it.

I'm not sure how much longer I can be surrounded by all the pictures and memories of my childhood before I break down and try to reconnect with the old me. The younger, naïve, happy Nina used to lie on her back with her head hung over the side of the bed while chatting with her friends on the phone.

"Nina?"

I jump a little at the sound of my mom's voice. "Hi," I greet.

She's in black leggings and one of my dad's old college sweatshirts. Her hair is a replica of my own—an inch past her breasts, multidimensional brown and wavy. Meg Solace is the most beautiful woman I have ever seen.

She lingers in the doorway for a moment as she looks around my room. Where my gaze was calculating, hers is just plain sad. I cock my head, watching her as she leaves, walks into my bathroom across the hall, and returns carrying a purple tote.

"I don't need that, Mom," I argue as she places it in an empty box by my closet. She doesn't say anything, just meanders over and sits beside me against the wall. I sigh. "That's not my thing anymore."

"No?" Mom challenges with a cocked brow. "Then what is your *thing*, Nina?"

I stiffen and drop my gaze. "I don't know, I guess."

She hums softly in the silence of my bedroom. *I can't believe I'm moving out in a week.* "Then start with painting your nails, sweetie. Come on, now, you can't let that entire bag of nail polish and nail files go to waste."

"I'm sure they expired long ago, Mom."

I cringe, realizing how dark that comment really was. The truth is I haven't painted my nails since the night before my sweet sixteen. The night before a monster kidnapped me. I remember the maroon color like it was only yesterday because I would wonder some days if I was seeing my blood or the polish.

My mom's answering gulp is loud in the sad silence. "Are you going to be okay?"

A choked laugh puffs out of me before I can control the urge to cry. The tears fall freely from my eyes, pulling my head down to rest on my momma's shoulder. "I can cook and clean. I'm very good at staying out of trouble too," I tease morbidly.

"God, Nina," Mom cries, swatting my knee gently. "It's not funny."

"Sorry," I mutter, even if we both know it's true. Mom and Dad know most of what I endured from the ages of sixteen through eighteen.

I learned really fast that if I didn't cook and clean properly or quick enough, I wouldn't be able to breathe properly, let alone move easily the following days. The beatings I took taught me to stay out of trouble and follow orders.

The urge to joke that I'll make an amazing employee because of what Mr. M taught me is strong, but I'd rather not upset Mom any more than I usually do. It's true, though. I was trained to serve the most vile of creatures, so getting a job with a half decent boss should be easy. I'll keep my house clean and feed my parents whenever they come to visit.

"You'll remember to eat?" I nod at my mom's wobbly question. "And no food before bed."

I nod again. "I know. It makes the nightmares worse." All that means is we've learned that I scream louder if I have a snack right before I go to sleep.

"I love you so much, baby. I'm so proud of you." She sniffles and kisses the top of my head.

Another couple of tears fall as I soak in her eternal love and warmth. "I know. I love *you*."

"Anything you need, I'm there."

"Me too," my dad adds from the doorway with a gentle smile on his face as he watches me and his wife snuggle.

I nod, knowing they're being honest. Our love is that of soulmates. If something like that exists, then my mom and I share a bond across all planes of existence. My dad is our eternal cheerleader and sidekick.

No matter how far I go, or how much they encourage me out of the nest, they will forever be my heart and soul. I'm afraid I'll plummet because I'm pretty sure my wings are broken beyond repair.

Chapter 5

Kai

I'm one of those people who doesn't need an alarm to wake up at the ass crack of dawn. I think of it as a good quality, but really there's no way for me to get back to sleep once my dreams scramble my brain.

A bonus to my early morning restlessness is that the trails are usually pretty quiet. Honestly, I might appreciate *and* ignore the fact that my obvious trauma of losing my best friend aids a damn good hobby.

I bite back a groan as I stretch my arms above my head. On my exhale, I turn on my side and wiggle my way over to Henry. He's much further away than we ever sleep. Worry courses through me. Henry is generally an introspective person, but sometimes he gets trapped in there; held hostage by his emotions. Ridge's drawing last night sent Henry into a quiet tailspin that will be difficult to pull him out of.

Ignoring his tight ass against my morning wood, I wrap my left arm around his waist and tug him gently so as not to wake him. I startle when bloodshot blue eyes connect with mine.

"Baby..." I whisper, my heart cracking at the pain I feel radiating off of him.

"Morning," he croaks.

Christ, he looks so tired, and I don't mean just physically. My fiancé's *soul* is tired. I pepper a few kisses on his splotchy cheeks. "Why are you awake, Henry?"

In the soft glow of our bedroom from the nightlight, I watch his attention flick to the picture that's been at our bedside for years. He shrugs while my throat tightens with emotion.

It feels like just yesterday Nina wrapped her arms around mine and Henry's necks, then jumped up so we could swing her between us. She was always so much smaller than us. *I miss the way she used to climb us like a little monkey.*

"Kai—"

"I know," I soothe. Looking at the last photo we have of her makes the urge to tug the blanket over us and never face the world again that much stronger. "I know, baby."

He sighs and wiggles against me to roll back onto his side. "Does something feel different lately to you?"

I frown into his bare shoulder. "What do you mean?"

"I mean..." He's silent for a moment. "Like something's about to change." Running my lips across his smooth skin, I shake my head. "What if it's Nina?"

This isn't the first time we've had this kind of conversation. I'm not sure what triggers this feeling in Henry, but I try to be supportive. He's always been different, more in tune with...something. The universe maybe? Fate? Who knows, but I believe him when he expresses these things.

"It's been a while since you felt like this." It's not a question, but a prompt for him to explain himself more. The curiosity and anxiety I experience each time scares me, like I too feel something shifting in the world. All it took to notice it was my fiancé pointing it out.

"Over a year and a half ago," he confirms, still looking at the picture beside our bed. "I thought maybe..."

I know what he thought. For an entire month, Henry had the volume on his phone as high as it could go. He rarely let his cell out of his sight just in case we got the call we've been waiting for since we were sixteen and seventeen. Nina's mom and dad promised to call us if anything ever changed with Nina's case.

Leaving our hometown was the hardest thing we've ever done aside from losing the heart of our group. It felt like admitting defeat, as if moving on with our lives as adults meant giving up hope on Nina.

I admit, and I fucking *hate* that I feel this way, but my hope has taken some brutal hits over the years. Bouts of depression and indescribable guilt have taken chunks out of the four of us.

It's so hard not to follow the others into the pit of despair when it flares up. We're close, closer than friends. The four of us are a family. Losing Nina brought us together and forced us, as teenagers, to hold on to each other tighter. It never occurred to me and Henry to move out after I proposed last year. We're right where we're meant to be and if a couple living in a house with two other men is weird to some people, they can go fuck themselves.

We have a built-in support system and when times get rough, like now, we're damn lucky to have our best friends, our brothers, down the hall. Well, not down the hall; upstairs. They don't need to hear me fucking my man until the sheets don't muffle his screams.

Turning my head to my wrist, I take a deep inhale. My breath stutters at the absence of her scent.

"Here," Henry says, sounding a bit more alive in the face of my desperation for our girl. I keep my forehead pressed into his shoulder blade even as I hear the beep of him turning the humidifier on. "Up."

Heeding his demand, I lift my head and let him maneuver me until we're facing my side of the bed with me as the little spoon now.

"Breathe, love."

I take a breath and immediately release a sigh of relief when the scent of roses settles my nerves. Nina always smelled like roses. *I wonder if she tasted like them too.*

After a while of us soaking in the aroma from my humidifier, Henry slides his hand from my stomach to my hip. "Stay with me this morning?"

My dick twitches. I roll to my back, groaning as the sheets tease the sensitive tip. He doesn't hesitate to twirl his rough fingers through the patch of hair at the base of my cock. The sadness that strangled me minutes before, settles into a weight passed on to the shoulders of the entire family.

"Have I ever denied you anything?" I grin when his eyes light up.

"Does that mean I can have your mouth?"

Fuck the hike. I'm gonna follow his happy trail instead.

Chapter 6

Nina

"How are you feeling about tomorrow, sweetie?"

The garlic bread in my mouth tastes like ash. *How am I feeling? I feel sick to my stomach and petrified.*

Peeking up at my mom, I try not to let her worried expression rub off on me more than it already has. I shrug and ask a question of my own. "Are you guys excited?"

My tone comes off sad, not sassy, thankfully. If there's anything that would upset my dad, it would be disrespecting my mom. Still, my mom's fork clatters to her plate and her hand flies to her chest. Her reaction has me pausing and finally getting a good look at her.

"Nina, I'm *terrified*," she says aghast, like she can't believe I would ever think they would be happy to be empty nesters finally.

"Meg—" my dad mutters.

Mom shoots him a hard look while wiping tears from her cheeks. "No, Will. She needs to know how we feel about her leaving."

26

This, *this* is why I think they'll be happy to have me moved out. All I ever do is cause tension and turmoil. Sometimes I wonder if I was better off never coming home or fighting for freedom. *Mom cries so much because of me.*

"I know, darling, but maybe not at the dinner table." Dad's trying to be reasonable, but the damage is done. Mom and I won't be finishing our dinner. My fears may be crippling since surviving Mr. M, but Mom and I have always lived with anxiety.

"It's fine, Dad."

He turns to me and gives me a quivering smile. "My sweet girl. We're scared too. We don't want you to leave ever, but it really is time. It's time to push ourselves outside of our new normal. We would be holding you back if we didn't encourage you to find what makes you happy again."

"I know," I reply, my monotone voice making his salt and pepper eyebrows furrow. I get it, I really do. If they weren't pushing me, I would stay here for the rest of my life, only being dragged to the grocery store once a month.

"I want you to be happy..." Mom whispers with tears still running down her cheeks.

I haven't been happy for a long time. In fact, I can remember the last time I felt joy so vividly.

⸻

"D*o you like it?"*

"*Ridge, oh my god!" The squeal that bursts out of me doesn't do my excitement justice in any way. "This is amazing!"*

I run around his office/art studio in wonder. I can't believe he's showing me this! *I stop in front of five sets of stunning eyes hung on the wall.*

"Ridgie, these are beautiful," *I hum, taking in all the finite details and additions of colors he added to each eyeball.*

Spinning in a circle, I try my best to keep my ego in check when I notice how many portraits he has of me hung and strewn across his ridiculously sized desk.

"I was wondering..." *He coughs while rubbing the back of his neck. His messy strawberry blond hair gives him an air of nervousness, and the meticulous way he readjusts his sexy glasses makes my neck tingle.*

I take a step toward him, really freaking hoping he's going to ask me what I want all four of my guys to ask. Why else would he bring me into his secret room? "Wondering what?"

"Do you want to make one with me?"

Disappointment flares hard and fast, but I push it away, then attempt to lighten the mood. "A baby?"

Ridge sputters, then lunges for me, making me squeak and try to bolt away. "No, heathen!" *Before I can get very far, he snatches the back of Trevor's sweatshirt I'm wearing.* "I want you to make something with me. Like a project that's all ours."

Sounds like he wants to make a baby with me. Instead of teasing him when it's clear he's showing me his most vulnerable side, I smile up at him. Jeez, they've all grown like a weed this year. "I would love to. But let's stick to our skills, so it turns out good."

He beams at me, and I can see his mind whirring with possibilities of what we could make. I'm not incredibly artsy like Ridge is, but I'm decent with some charcoal and no clear rules. He's my color man...Always making things brighter and beautiful.

After a while of him letting me poke through his stuff, he taps me on the hip. "Are you happy, Neen?"

I smile. I would be happier if he would take my first kiss, but we'll get there someday. *Showing me all of this is the equivalent of him ripping his heart and soul out, then letting me prod at them.* "This is the best birthday gift, Ridgie."

He smiles right back at me. "Happy sweet sixteen, Nina."

W OOF!
　　NO.

Pain flares in my knees where I slam them into the bottom of the table.

"Shit! Nina, you're okay. Just someone walking by."

I hear my dad's voice, but his words don't make any sense, nor do they matter. I'm shaking and breathing fast enough to make my head swim and my chest ache.

"Breathe, sweetie."

No. I can't breathe. Logic battles the fear pumping through my veins. I scramble from the table to check out each window as sneakily as I can until I'm sure the monster and his hellhound aren't outside waiting to take another chunk of my soul and flesh. A sniffle behind me has me deflating.

"I'm going to bed," I whisper, hating myself so dang much that I can't even look at my parents as I climb the stairs.

My last night home and I ruined it.

Chapter 7

Henry

I know I need to stop imagining what Nina would say about my rock wall, but it's hard. The pink quartz ones were always her favorite. That's why I have an entire shelf dedicated to the ones I know she would love.

Those are for sure the prettiest, but I've found some cool shapes over the years in simple blacks and browns. I wonder what she would say about those. Nina would definitely like my small collection of heart-shaped ones.

Rock collecting doesn't actually interest me, never has, but I can recall the joy on Nina's face every time she added a rock to her collection. Rocks are just chunks of earth to me, so why do I have one hundred and ninety-eight stones in my bedroom? Because I can vividly imagine Nina's face every time I pick one up.

I'm collecting her source of happiness. Many times, like right now, I don't feel that surge of warmth. I feeling fucking sad.

"Hey, man."

I nudge my foot against my desk and spin until I see Trevor leaning against the doorframe of my office. "Hey."

His eyes narrow at my tired tone. "You alright?"

Shrugging, I lean back in my chair just as Kai shouts and Ridge laughs loudly from the kitchen down the hall. I should be out there with them, making dinner together like we do every Friday night, but I just can't get out of my head.

Enter Trevor.

"How's your next project coming along?"

I laugh a little, knowing he was sent in to distract me and fix me up. Not much can get me out of my slump, but Trevor has a knack for knowing what I need. Even Kai isn't as good as Trev.

Glancing behind me at the book laid out on my tabletop, I grimace. "Been a bit distracted."

Trev kicks off the door and comes to see the lack of progress I've made on this restoration. "How old is it?"

Frowning, I spin to look at it again and try to remember what my client told me about it. "Christ," I groan and rub my hand down my face. "I don't know off the top of my head, but the binding needs some serious work. It isn't just old, it's damaged too."

"Usual guy?"

I nod. Restoring books is slow paying if you don't know the right people. Unfortunately, I don't have the equipment or space to restore super old books, and without that stuff, I would do more harm than good. The man Trev's referring to finds old books with his wife when they travel. He's filled my pockets nicely.

"Any special edition covers?" Trevor asks softly, taking care not to touch anything on my desk as he studies my work.

I shake my head. "Not at the moment. This guy brought me

six back from his most recent trip, so I'm focusing on them right now."

My talents with books are pretty vast, so often I love to lose myself in creating a cool special edition piece—not electronically. With good leather and a steady hand, there's some cool shit I can do.

Trev steps back and drops a hand on my shoulder. "Come make dinner with us. It will make you feel better."

I sigh and roll my head on my shoulders. He's right. It's the same for all four of us; the longer we wallow alone, the worse we'll get. "You're right."

"Obviously," he jokes, pulling on my sleeve until I'm standing. Trevor pulls me out of the office and only releases me once the door has snicked shut behind us. "You know we always got you, right?"

"I know," I agree and give my friend a grateful smile. Ridge and Trevor may be the only blood relatives in our group of four, but we're family through and through.

My entrance into the open concept kitchen that flows into our dining room and living room doesn't go unnoticed by Kai. "Hey, baby," he murmurs, swooping in to give me a scorching kiss.

The blood rushing to my dick screeches to a painful halt when Ridge cries out in mock disgust. "HEY! MY *EYES!*"

Kai tugs me into him a bit harder and grins against my mouth. I chuckle and pull back before I let him have his wicked way with me.

"Idiot," Trevor mutters, shoving Ridge out of the way to stir a pot of sauce on the burner.

"Get a room," Ridge grumbles as Kai takes a nip of my collarbone.

To my utter embarrassment, Kai says, "But Henry loves being bent over the island."

"NO!" Ridge gasps, appalled. His face turns red, but definitely not as red as mine.

Trevor sighs by the fridge now. "Guys—" His phone ringing cuts his reprimand off.

My stomach bottoms out for reasons I'm terrified of analyzing. "Speakerphone," I croak. I know in my gut that whoever is on the other end of that phone call is about to turn our world upside down.

Chapter 8

Nina

My fridge is stocked, there's taco meat on the stove, and I'm in no mood for company, so really, there's no reason my mom can find to stay. We both know the next step is literally her walking out my front door.

I hate it so much. My throat aches with the strength it's taking to hold my sobs inside. I want my dad to stay. I want my mom to come sit on my pretty burnt orange couch and watch our favorite vampire show.

My god, I want them to stay so badly I feel like my chest is going to concave any minute now. Dad's already outside, having hugged me minutes ago. I'll hold on to his parting words forever, just like I did when I was locked in that basement.

Whether it's a phone call right before I'm kidnapped, or leaving me to get settled into my new home alone, he always ensures his final words are *I love you, sweet.*

My mom, though? She breaks my heart in a different kind of way. It's the pure love and devotion in her watery eyes that makes the urge to crumble to the ground, then beg her to stay all that more powerful.

I know I reflect the same emotions in my gaze and that's why she's hesitating to leave. Mom and I are the same and when heavy emotions are involved, we're like a live wire ready to explode in a puddle of tears.

Crying never used to be my default, but these past few years, even when I'm numb, my tears have been my only outlet. Sometimes I'll be so disassociated to what's going on in my mind that I don't realize my chin is dripping with salty despair.

That's when Mom and Dad get the most worried. In my disconnect there's so much unknown. *Too* much.

Therapy has helped me learn my triggers, but I fear my trauma is so irreparable that awareness won't do me any good. I can usually feel the panic coming on and pinpoint why, but there's no going back. The current is too strong. The *trauma* is too consuming.

That's why I'm a homebody. Avoiding everything is safer. Thank goodness for all the new delivery services. The only apps downloaded on my phone are for food. Every subscription I have is to keep me at home. I have movies, TV shows, and games thanks to my old PS4.

I'll be happy enough with Zombies and chocolate-covered almonds for the rest of my life if it means ignoring the world.

"I love you, Nina. Please, *please* call me before you go to bed."

Nodding at my mom, I refrain from telling her I don't currently know where my phone is. It's somewhere in this house that echoes with emptiness. Even with all of my boxes unpacked and the new *everything* my parents filled it with, family photos included, I swear it still echoes.

After the sheer chaos of my mom decorating and making my entire home look already lived in after a short forty-eight hours, of course I have no idea where the heck she docked my phone, but I don't really care.

"I will. Love you, Mom," I whisper, hoping she doesn't hear the crack in my voice. No such luck; her lip wobbles. She takes a step toward me, but Dad halts her in her tracks.

"Meg, darling," he coos softly, stopping just outside my front door. Behind him, my quiet, cozy neighborhood glows in the desert sunset of Provo, Utah. "It's time to go."

"But—"

Darting forward, I cut her off and slam my smaller body into hers. I never did surpass her 5'9" curvy frame. Years of malnourishment and PTSD keep me far thinner than anyone would consider sexy. I'm nothing but a 5'6" waif in my mom's trembling arms.

"I love you, Mom." I don't tell her I'll be okay, because I don't think I will. But I can express with all my heart that I love her and show her in my tight hold how much I'll miss her.

Her answering words shatter me. "I'm proud of you, sweetie." And her parting statement puts me back together as she steps out of my new home. "I love you. Always and forever."

"Always and forever," I choke out and when the door closes behind her, I become weightless. My knees crashing into the hardwood floors jar my teeth and shake my sobs free.

If anyone has the ability to make me love so much it breaks me, it's my mom. And quoting our favorite show solidifies that I didn't realize how much I would actually miss her until this moment.

That same sorrow shoots adrenaline through my wobbly limbs, allowing me to stand and rush for my bay window. I watch my dad guide my mom into the passenger seat of their Lexus, and when he kisses her gently as he buckles her in, I can't stop my smile.

Memorizing their features like it could be the last time I see them, I study the way my mom wipes her cheeks and rummages around in her purse. Dad nods at her when he gets into the driver's seat and starts the car.

I so badly want to be with them. Rarely do I add my own thoughts to their conversations, but to just bask in their presence is healing.

My eyebrows relax and my lips part on a sigh as I witness the normalcy that are my parents. *Take me with you*, I want to shout, but I hold it in. If they think this is best, then I'll trust them, but only because I agree they deserve an empty nest after everything I've put them through.

The relaxation I feel takes a nosedive into a deep frown when Mom presses her phone to her ear. *Who's she calling?*

Jolting at the sound of the oven letting me know it's preheated for my tortillas, I turn away from the window. My appetite is crap, but I can always make an effort for a taco.

Chapter 9

Trevor

I can't explain the reason my heart drops beyond trusting Henry's instincts. Whatever he's feeling at the sound of my ringtone has the blood draining from his face. And because my friend is already a pale guy, well, let's just say I'm fucking terrified of the picture he's painting.

Where Henry looks like he's about to pass out, Ridge hasn't looked away from my cell on the island between us. Kai's eyes are darting around like he's not understanding our reaction, but when he reaches for my phone, I bark at him to stop.

I can't tell who or what is on the other side of the line, but if I can shield my brothers from it, I will. Shoving my hesitation to the recesses of my mind, I snatch the device.

"Speakerphone," Henry pleads in a voice so monotone it makes the hair on the back of my neck stand on end.

Glancing at the other two, they nod mutely, making my decision to protect them from this null. I swipe to accept the call.

"Trevor speaking." *Please, for the love of fuck, let there be a flood in one of the bathrooms at one of our hotels.*

No such luck.

My stomach twists itself even tighter when a sniffle adds to the mystery of the unknown number.

I clear my throat. "Hello?"

"T-Trevor, honey? Is that y-you?"

Ridge stumbles away from the kitchen island, Kai gasps, and Henry stiffens. At the sound of Meg Solace's voice, I wobble. My free hand is the only thing that catches me while my phone clatters onto the counter.

"Trevor?"

Everything in me screams for the man I once considered more like a father to me than my own blood. I want to shout at Will and demand why he stopped answering my calls.

"Son?"

At that, I grunt. "Will?"

"Shit, Trev. I'm so sorry. So, so damn sorry," Nina's dad says gruffly, all the while I can hear his wife's cries in the background. *Or maybe it's Nina?*

"Where—" I can't ask.

Kai steps forward. "Is—" He too stumbles over his words.

Do we even want to know?! How fucking horrible are we to second guess if we actually want the update we've been waiting for all these years?!

Henry swallows repeatedly like he can't get his voice to function.

Will breaks the tense silence with soft understanding. "Are you all there?"

To my surprise, Ridge steps forward, not even taking a moment to wipe the tears from his cheeks. "Where is Nina, Mr. Solace?"

Silence. Then there's quiet murmuring before Will finally responds. "Can we meet? Please. We're in town and can go wherever is easiest."

I frown. "Where are you?"

"Provo," comes Will's immediate response.

"We moved a year ago. We're in St. George," I explain.

"About three and a half hours away," Henry mutters trying his damnedest to rip his hair out of his skull as he paces.

"Henry?!" Meg makes herself known again. "Oh my...I've missed you."

Henry looks like he's about to shatter completely when Kai swoops in to give him a giant hug of support.

Cursing draws my attention back to this nightmarish conversation. *What aren't they telling us?!*

Ridge seems ready to snap, so before he can, I bolt around the counter and place a heavy hand on his shoulder. He's our short fuse and I'm our rock.

"Drink," I state, not giving my cousin room to argue when I shove a bottle of Gatorade into his trembling hand. It's time I take charge; it's what I do best. What I *enjoy*.

"Tell me, Will. Now."

My fingers dig into Ridge's shoulder when the silence drags on. A sputtering breath and another whimper sound from my phone.

"It's Nina..." Will whispers because he knows our world's just imploded. "She's—"

My throat closes over, ready to save myself from digesting the worst possible news. *Did they find her body?* The police always were quick to assume she was dead after so many years of a cold trail.

"Nina's..."

"WILL!" I shout, my emotions erupting in a bout of frustration and fear. "Where is our Nina?!"

"In Provo," Will gasps out like he too can't hold himself together any longer. "She-she needs you."

Kai lunges for the phone and asks what we've been wondering for so fucking long. "Nina's alive?!"

The moment we've all been waiting for is finally here, and I'm not ready to live it because what if the person I've loved most in the world is gone? And what if she isn't? What then?

Will stutters over his life altering words. "Y—" My heart thumps an extra beat, then another until I'm all but hyperventilating and giving Ridge all my weight. "Yes. Nina is a-alive."

ALIVE! OUR NINA IS ALIVE!

Chapter 10

Ridge

"R idge..." Trevor's tone holds enough warning to draw my attention. "You need to calm down."

"Calm down?" *CALM DOWN?!* "The fuck you mean I need to calm down?" I snarl. It takes a tremendous amount of effort not to attack him right now and the only reason I haven't yet is because he's the one driving the fucking truck.

"We're almost there, man."

I hate the understanding in my cousin's voice. He doesn't fucking get it. "We would already be there if you had let *me* drive, asshole! How are you going the speed limit knowing Nina's there?!"

It was almost four when Trevor's phone rang, and it was around 4:45 P.M. when we rushed out of the house with all of our essentials. Nina's in Provo, so that's where we will be for the foreseeable future. Fuck our house. We have resorts all over Utah, we can stay in those.

"And get us into an accident or pulled over?" Trev shoots

me a look, then glances in the rearview mirror to check on Kai and Henry.

Taking separate cars didn't bother me since I would have double the opportunity to leave them behind and find my girl if they had a different opinion. What *does* annoy the living shit out of me is how slow we're going.

Finally, the *Neen's Resorts* sign comes into view. I have no headspace to admire what Trev and I have done with our business because as soon as we pull up to the valet, I'm out of the car in a flash with Henry hot on my heels.

At least someone shares my sense of urgency.

"Shit!" I hear Kai curse, most likely worried about his fiancé bolting away from him.

Bypassing the revolving doors, Henry and I shove through the normal ones. My heart pounds and I feel like I'm not getting enough air in my lungs, but it doesn't matter. All that matters is that Nina's in the cozy conference room down the main hall.

"Ridge," Henry gasps like he's struggling to control his emotions. I don't respond. Instead, I shove my shoulder into the wide wooden door as I unlatch the handle.

"Nina!" I stumble to a stop, not understanding what I'm seeing. Will is standing by the coffee table and partially covering his wife who has a hand to her chest. They look startled, but I can't find it in me to care right now. Just like I ignore the extra grays in Will's hair and the weathered look of Meg's trembling hand. All I care about it the absence of Nina. "Where is she?"

Will frowns. "She's not here." His words are greeted with two additional snarls of discontent as Trevor and Kai rush into the room.

"Why the f—"

"Ridge!" Trevor snaps, nudging me to the side so he can

reach the people we once considered family. Then they went and left us hanging in hell years ago.

"Trevor," Nina's mom whispers, standing and staring wide eyed at my cousin. "You've grown. My goodness, I've missed you. All of you." Her attention shifts between all four of us and my anger with her fades a little.

Wrapping her in a hug, Trevor murmurs something in her ear. When he pulls away to shake Will's hand, Kai swoops in for a hug and hushed words. Henry isn't far behind, but he's a bit more hesitant than the other two. When the three of them are done greeting, my brothers and Nina's parents stare at me, waiting for me to forgive and forget.

My rage has simmered, but the hurt still burns. "Where is she?" I ask again. The energy in the room charges again when Meg and Will exchange a painful glance. "Please. *Please,* fucking tell me."

I'll get on my knees if it means we finally get the truth. Anything to know where my Nina is, and what happened.

"Sit, honey," Meg murmurs, gesturing to the other couches. Grinding my jaw, I do as she asks and sit beside Trev. She doesn't waste any more time, seeming to have composed herself. "Nina's okay. We just moved her into her own home."

"Moved her in—what?" Kai's confusion matches my own.

Henry sits forward with a deep frown bunching the freckles around his nose. "Back up. She was missing for four years and suddenly she's moving into her own house?"

The parents glance at each other *again.* My temper sparks, but Will douses my flame with cold water. "It wasn't sudden, son. Nina was only missing for two years."

Chaos erupts around me, but my brothers' horrified shouts have nothing on the way my heart plummets and shatters into a million tiny little pieces. My vision tunnels until all I can see are my white-knuckled fists.

"ENOUGH!" Will bellows, effectively yanking me out of the trance I was in. "You will *not* behave this way in front of my wife. Do you understand me?!"

"Fuck," Trevor mutters. "*Fuck...*I'm sorry, Meg."

He continues pacing the length of the room, only serving to heighten my anxiety. Trev's our calm one...our caretaker and leader. Seeing him so distraught does nothing to help my torrent of emotions.

The urge to throw up is curbed by Kai's next question because if I puke, we won't get the answers we need right away. "What...Where has she been for the past two and a half years?"

"Maybe we should revisit—"

I can't hold back any longer. Jumping from the couch, I point my finger at Will and cut him off. "No!"

A hand slams down on my offending one, then Kai comes into view and nudges me back by my shoulders. I open my mouth to scream at him, but the tears in his eyes have me backing off. "Let Henry," Kai whispers.

Peeking behind him, I see Henry stand and repeat Kai's question. "Where has she been, Mr. Solace? Please. We have to know. To *see* her, at least."

I didn't think my heart could hurt after its brutal assassination not five minutes ago, but Henry sends a spark of pain through my chest with his broken plea.

So help me God, if they glance at each other one more time...

Nina's mom leans forward on the edge of her seat and steals our breath away with her explanation. "The first year she was in inpatient care. For the past year and a half, she's been at home. Healing."

Healing?

Meg lifts her gaze and looks me dead in the eye as she eviscerates my soul. "I called Ridge a few days after she was found, but you changed your number."

The ringing is back, and my knees suddenly ache. I barely hear the rest, but the words still hammer my brain like the torture I deserve.

"I planned to try Kai next, but once we saw the true extent of Nina's...struggles...we thought it was best to allow her to heal first before bringing more people in."

Two and a half years.

It's all my fault.

Every. Single. Thing.

The kidnapping.

Not being there to help her heal.

All. My. Fault.

"She needs you guys."

I don't know the context or who's even speaking. All I know is she needed me, *past tense*, and I failed at every turn.

Is there any coming back from my mistakes?

Chapter 11

Nina

How does a normal young adult react when their parents admit that they booked a hotel room for a *week* instead of the three days they told me at first? *A week!*

My dilemma comes from the fact that they lied and stayed to keep an eye on me, but I'm secretly so freaking happy to see them on my front step. So what do I do? I open the door wide and allow them inside.

With all the locks in place, I turn around and place my hands on my hips with confidence I don't feel. "So you're here for four more days?"

Mom nods happily while Dad meanders into my kitchen. He opens the fridge and immediately frowns. "It looks the same, Nina."

I sigh, my stance deflating. "I saw you yesterday. And I'm one small person."

"Let's go out for dinner." Mom claps excitedly, trying to diffuse the tension.

Something's off with them, but I don't have the energy to

47

figure it out. I didn't sleep well last night. Actually, I haven't slept well in four and a half years. I'm perpetually exhausted.

Nibbling the inside of my cheek, I fidget while trying to figure out how to say no. My parents have rarely pushed me outside of my comfort zone. *Encouraging* me to move out was the biggest nudge of all, and now they what? Want me to sit in a small space with a bunch of strangers watching me while I *don't* eat?

"Nina?"

I step back and around my mom, not wanting her pitying touches and looks. "I'm not hungry," I mutter, barely able to control myself from running to the corner of my couch.

The open concept is great when I need space, but more often than not, I like to *know* without a doubt that I'm alone and nobody can find me. I've been eyeing up the little nook under the stairs and debating if I can make it into a cozy space when I need it. Plus, the door is incredibly discreet.

I want to hide. From my mom. Dinner. From the world. Tugging my blanket up to my chin, I curl into the couch, then watch as my mom and dad approach me. Mom sits by my feet, and Dad drapes another blanket around me before kissing my forehead.

"Take a nap, sweet. We'll watch over you. Just rest now."

I'll never sleep as well as I do when my dad assures me of his protection. So as my mom turns our vampire show on for the millionth time and puts the volume on low, I allow myself to drift off into a dreamless sleep.

Hushed voices are the first thing I notice as I wake. Blinking, I rub away the sleepiness from my eyes and take in how cozy my living room is. I must have slept through the rest of the day, because now it's dark, but the warm lighting from the dining room and kitchen are creating a gentle hue around my living room.

The TV is still quiet, and it looks like the main bad boy vampire is carrying his girlfriend to safety. *Yum.*

"You shouldn't be here!" I hear dad hiss. Immediately, I stiffen and look around, only to realize Mom and Dad are nowhere to be seen. More muttering. "No. You need to leave."

A lump forms in my throat and my belly twists uncomfortably. *Who's here?* A thud sounds, then Mom becomes partially visible behind the wall that separates the entryway and the living room. She looks pale and anxious, freaking me out even more. But Dad's next words send me spiraling.

"No. Seriously, you all need to leave. Nina's not ready for this."

Vomit crawls up my throat, but gravity shoves it back down as I jump up from the couch and sprint to the one place I think I'll be safe. *Someone's here. People are here! For* me.

As quietly as my shaking body can allow, I yank the small door open by its tiny brass latch and sneak into the stairwell nook. I don't even care if there's no handle to get out from the inside. All that matters is I can control this space. Mom and Dad know about this spot, but I hope they forget about it.

Please, please, please, leave me alone!

Chapter 12

Kai

"**Y**ou shouldn't be here!"

Fuck. I expected Will's reaction to us intercepting the pizza delivery man and showing up with their dinner unannounced, but I didn't prepare myself for the tantalizing scent of rose drifting from the open doorway.

She still smells the same.

A strangled sound erupts from my throat, but I rein myself in when Henry squeezes my hip.

"Will, please. We need to see her," Trev begs quietly with his hands splayed in front of him like he's trying to prove he's not a threat.

Will shakes his head. "No. You need to leave."

We don't move an inch. If anything, I'm eager to keep moving forward until I can finally lay eyes on my girl.

"Boys..." Meg murmurs, glancing behind her.

"Please, Mrs. Solace!" Ridge pleads desperately, trying to push Trev to the side, most likely to force his way into Nina's house.

My grip on the two pizza boxes tightens when Meg steps

50

back with a hand to her chest and looking pale. Will stiffens and straightens his broad shoulders even more. Trev also glares at his cousin.

"Ridge," Henry whispers, tugging on our friend's shirt to protect him from himself. *Fucking hell, he scared Nina's mom.*

I watch warily as Nina's dad takes a deep breath and unclenches his fists. "No. Seriously, you all need to leave. Nina's not ready for this."

Unable to hold myself back any longer, I swallow and say, "Sir—"

Just then, a flash of brown darts behind Meg and disappears from view. "Nina!" I gasp, lurching forward with no resistance as Trevor and Ridge brush past Mr. Solace.

Stumbling after them, I'm slammed with a glorious wall of rose and coziness as I take in Nina's new home. The only problem with her space is that she's nowhere to be found.

"Where did she go?!" Ridge demands, turning in a circle in her entryway. He's flushed and flustered, clearly struggling with the concept of moving further.

Not realizing Trevor had disappeared too, I jump when he comes running back around the corner and takes a step toward the staircase to the right of us.

"Don't take another step young man," Will snarls, having stepped in front of Trevor the moment he realized where he was headed. "You're violating her space."

"We are not," Trevor growls back like a beast ready to go to battle for the woman he loves. "You know we love her. We would never violate her in *any* fucking way!"

Meg shifts out of the corner of my eye and it's then I realize Henry is already following Nina's mom. *Does she know where Nina's hiding?* Will's stopping Trev from going upstairs. *Did she run up there?*

Why was she running?

So many questions, yet Trevor and Will are still arguing over boundaries.

Meg slips behind the fuming alpha men with Henry shifting and maneuvering so Will doesn't notice. As much as I'd like to see where Meg's going, I don't move, knowing it will only draw attention to them. If Nina's dad is going to keep us from her, and Henry is sneaking around to see if Meg can find Nina, I'll just have to wait.

Ridge, on the other hand, seems ready to throw up. I figured he would be the one to go in guns blazing and declaring his undying love for Nina, but since stepping into a space that so clearly screams *Nina,* he's frozen.

Henry's shocked question snaps us all out of vastly different trances. "She's under the stairs?!"

At that, I drop the pizza boxes as gently as I can, my priorities taking a turn. I bolt around Ridge and the other two men, my heart thundering in my chest. Meg kneels in front of the wall below the staircase with her mouth dropped wide open. "Gosh, Henry. You scared the daylights out of me!"

"Damn it! Out of my way," Will grumbles, then pushes me and Henry aside. Crouching down beside his wife, he reaches for the wall and fiddles with something until there's an audible click.

I watch as this big protective dad takes a shuddering breath and opens the hidden door that can't be more than three feet tall. He cracks it enough to peek inside, then curses softly before closing it again.

Trevor makes a pained noise, also having snuck a glance over Will's head. "I can help her. Let me in," he says, almost begging now.

Will's head thunks into the door, shaking it sadly for a moment. When he leans back, he sighs. "You can't help her right now. Only Meg can. Go take a seat, boys. We need to have a conversation."

Now I want to throw up. *What the hell is going on?*

I feel them moving around me, but I can't take my eyes off the door Meg just disappeared into. She's in there; Nina's in there. Mere feet away and it feels utterly impossible to move an inch in the opposite direction.

"Kai. Come sit, brother."

Even glancing over my shoulder to see Trevor holding out a chair for me is painful. The anxious look on my fiancé's face is what convinces me into that seat. Henry needs me, and fuck, I need him too. Especially considering Will looks like someone just killed his cat in front of him.

Nina's dad clears his throat and I swear my organs revolt. "We've told you Nina was missing for about two years, where she went after and when she came home. But you don't know what happened while she was gone."

"Tell us." Ridge sounds like he's dying, but still he stares Will down like he needs to hear every single horrific detail.

"Nina was forced to be many things in those two years and it's changed who she is. She's not the girl you used to know."

"Doesn't matter," Trevor states firmly.

Will stares him dead in the eye. "It matters more than you'll ever know. The Nina Meg and I have done our best to heal can't stand any sort of socialization. Noises and touch have to be monitored since she prefers the quiet and only prefers her mom to be near her."

Watching Nina's dad wipe away a stray tear scares me beyond words. *Touch...sound...socializing.* Nina was the loudest, most sociable, and physically affectionate girl I had ever met.

"She had rules. Clean, cook, and always do as she was told. She was malnourished, and it's been a battle for me and Meg to get her to eat." Her dad seems to zone out as he rattles off Nina's horrors in a pain-stricken tone. "Learning about the beatings and seeing all the scars should have been the worst part."

We all stiffen. *How could it get any fucking worse?! Jesus fucking Christ!!*

"But to hear your daughter tell her mother how she was forced to scrub her own pools of blood out of that bastard's rugs immediately following each whipping...That would break anyone."

"I'm going to be sick," Henry croaks and shoves away from the table, barely registering Will's pointed finger to the hallway where I'm assuming the bathroom is.

Trevor clears his throat, then swallows three times. "There's more, isn't there?"

Will nods. "That wasn't even scratching the surface, son."

Oh, Nina...

Chapter 13

Nina

Tingles race from the tip of my nose and through my upper lip, making the urge to itch incredibly agitating.

"Shh, sweetheart. Slowly now."

I feel my brows pull together as easily as I feel myself relax into my mom's lap. The tickles start on my forehead again and trail down my temples until it traces my ears.

"Mom," I murmur, unclenching my eyes as I come out of my panicked state. "When did you find me?"

She hums, her eyes damp with unshed tears. "Maybe five minutes ago. This was a bad one, Nina."

I nod as she continues to trace my features with her fingertips. She used to do this when I was little. Since coming home, it seems to be the only thing to pull me out of a panic attack without making it worse. I don't need deep breathing exercises or a cold shower. I just need my mom.

We study each other; me laying with my head in her lap and her looking down at me with so much love and worry it makes me feel guilty. Mom frowns and parts her lips before closing them again. I wait and when she whispers, "Do you trust me?" The hesitation in her voice forces me to remember there were people here for me. *To take me away?*

My breathing picks up and before I realize what's happening, I'm sitting with my knees pressed to my chest. "Who's here?"

"Nina. Do you trust me?" Mom's voice sounds firm, like she knows something awful I don't.

"Please. Don't let them take me away," I croak brokenly. Her mouth opens again but I rush on. "No, Mom. I'll do better. Don't let them take me."

I want to stay. I want to stay. I want to stay! I won't go back! I don't care if it's the basement or the institute. I won't go!

"Stop, sweetie."

She reaches for me, but I bury my head in my knees, crying and begging for her not to give up on me.

"Trevor. Henry. Ridge and Kai."

My breath catches. Those names...

Trevor, Henry, Ridge, and Kai.

Their names...

"All four of them are here."

Here? Why are they here?

"Because they want to see you," she answers my unspoken question. "They've missed you, sweetheart. We reached out to them yesterday and said you were okay."

I'm absolutely *not* okay. I'm rocking back and forth on my butt in a small closet under the stairs with my mom trying to calm me down like a wild animal.

"I know we all agreed to wait until you were ready, but Nina...It's time."

It's time. It's time. It's time. I HATE that statement. What about what *I* think about my time? I'm not ready. I'll never *be* ready because that part of my life is over. The happy parts are buried, and the bubbly parts of me they loved are broken. *POP!* Each whipping popped my bubbles that made me a joyful girl. I'm not ready and the guys are definitely never going to be ready to meet the new me.

"I think..."

Finally, I meet her gaze. "What?"

"I think they could help you," she says, but is that guilt I hear in her voice? "Sheesh Nina, I'm struggling here, okay? I wish I could keep you at home with me forever, but that would be so dang selfish of me. Encouraging you to grow and to explore the world again, explore who you are, that's what a mother is supposed to do."

If she cries, I'm gonna cry...

Sniffing, she quickly wipes her eyes before her tears can fall. "I want you to have support. I would love to be the only one you come to, but you're a woman now, sweetheart. An adult who needs more space to thrive. And those boys? They just trampled into this house because they love you so much. They will be good for you."

But will I be good for them? The answer is *no*, but if they're anything like I remember, the four of them are awfully stubborn. They will push and push until they get their eyes on me, then they'll see.

"Okay," I whimper quietly. The sooner I show them how broken I am, the sooner I'll be left alone.

Now it's Mom who hesitates. "A-are you sure? I didn't think you would—"

"It's fine." Why can't I speak louder than a whisper? At least the guys will get the full brunt of my issues. Shuffling to the corner, I wait for my mom to push the cracked door open first so I can hide behind her. *I never said I was mature.*

Still half bent over, Mom turns and pins me in place with

an intense stare. "If you don't want to, Nina, tell me. I'll kick them out with a frying pan."

I really don't want to. Smiling sadly, I shake my head. "Let's go."

I know she hates how little I talk, but telling her the truth would upset not only her but five other people as well. They want to see me. Mom wants me to see them, so I will. The most valuable thing I learned in my twenty-six months of captivity is that giving in is always the easiest option.

She eyes me for a moment longer, then moves to give me space to leave my nook. *I don't want to leave.* Panic threatens to send me crawling back inside and the suspense of the situation is only heightened by the pounding of the blood rushing in my ears.

Keeping my focus on my hands as I crawl, I try not to throw up. It's silent beyond the drums rattling inside my skull. Every ounce of willpower I have to keep moving forward dwindles with each breath I take.

A dust bunny swirling around my pinky finger soothes me just enough to take a steadying breath, and as I leave it behind to stand, I shift my attention to plucking at the fraying string on my shorts. My other hand goes to my chest in hopes that I can keep my heart inside if I press on it hard enough.

Don't look up, don't look up, I keep chanting. I love my open concept home, but right now, knowing everyone can see me makes me want to flee. Shifting to the left, I tuck myself behind Mom a little more as I try to gain control of myself.

My God...What is happening?! I can't do this. I CAN'T—

An audible gasp makes me jump and cower. "Neen?!"

That nickname, the one my guys coined and always spoke with warmth. It draws me up and out of my body, leaving my fizzing veins of nervousness behind if only so I could get one look at the boy who comforted me through every bump and bruise growing up.

Henry.

Tears blur my vision, but not before I realize that he's no longer a boy. Just as I am no longer a girl. *His girl. His Neen.* Time robbed me of seeing him grow into a man.

Four years and now his black hair is longer but still incredibly disheveled on top of his head. He's pale and his freckles have faded with maturity. He's painfully beautiful.

"Henry!" I choke out, reaching for him, *needing* him. But just as I planned, my body takes it upon itself to show him just how broken I truly am.

Darkness steals me from his embrace once again. My knees buckle and all feeling disappears before I feel the crash of my bones on the floor. Because that's all I am...skin and bones. Nothing to offer. I might as well be the dust bunny spinning in circles on the floor just waiting to be picked up and tossed out.

I'll be tossed out soon enough.

Chapter 14

Henry

I can't believe I threw up in Nina's bathroom. Not because I puked, though, but because I'm in *Nina's* bathroom. *She's here, she really is.*

I saw her blur by the door and I swear my heart doubled in size, readying to accommodate her once again. Not that she hasn't been in my heart all this time, but because I'm ready to add to the new version of the girl we all loved. *Love*, present tense because no matter how she's changed, Nina will always be our girl.

Unable to hold in my groan, I bend over the sink and suck some water into my mouth from the faucet. Swishing a few mouthfuls around, I spit and wipe my face clean with the bottom of my black T-shirt.

For a moment I enjoy the air conditioning breezing across my ankles and bare claves. Even in April, the average in Provo is like sixty-six degrees Fahrenheit—shorts are a must. Getting sick and having so much anxiety breathing hot air down my neck makes it so much worse.

Nina's home helps cool the stifling feel of my failures,

though. From the moment Will opened the door, the scent of my girl has tickled my nose. For years Kai has kept the smell of roses close, but nothing compares to the real thing: Nina. No candle, scent roller, diffuser, or air freshener can truly capture the pure essence that is Neen.

With one last tired look in the mirror, I take a deep breath. I know her dad has more to tell us and being scared to hear it won't change the outcome. I have to know what happened to Nina so I can help her. There is no universe or reality where I am not in her life.

We just found her again. She was never far from our thoughts and hearts. Now we won't allow her to be physically far from us ever again. We haven't talked about moving back to our college town, but it's obvious. We're staying with Nina.

The silence when I leave the bathroom makes my stomach knot uncomfortably. *Are the guys waiting for me? Fuck, now I've forced them to wait.*

Picking up speed, I hardly take in the photos lining the hallway or the extra two doors I pass, needing to break the suspense I can feel nipping at my heels.

I turn the corner and slowly come to a stop when I find Kai, Trev, and Ridge staring wide eyed toward my left. Will looks worried, and now I can't control my need to look. Bile crawls up my throat, the anticipation becoming too much. Stiffer than I thought possible, my whole body turns to see what has my family so shell-shocked.

Then I see her. My beautiful Nina.

I'm not sure what happens but my breath whooshes back down my throat, causing my eyes to burn. "Neen?!"

Neen, the girl we spent almost every waking moment laughing and playing with, is hiding behind Meg. When she turns, the stricken and absolute exhausted look dulling her stunning eyes almost brings me to my knees.

I'm not the one who collapses, though.

"Henry!"

The first time I hear Nina's voice in over four years brings a tsunami of relief and heartache that shoves me toward her just as she flings herself in my direction. I see the moment she loses herself, and I don't think it's something I'll ever be able to scrub from my mind. Those tortured eyes roll into the back of her head, and her arms which were reaching for me like I'm her lifeline go limp just as her knees buckle. Fear rushes up my throat and bursts out in a terrified curse.

"FUCK!"

The sickening crunch of her knees crashing into the floor makes my jaw clench and all my energy shift into ensuring she doesn't hurt herself further. As fast as I can, I sweep under her, ignoring the burning pain in my own bare knees to take the brunt of her weight on my chest and shoulders. *Fuck, that hurts.*

Grunting and shifting, I maneuver us until I have her cradled in my arms like a baby. My ears must be ringing, the panic having stolen one or two of my senses as I caught my girl, because next thing I know I have Kai's face inches from mine and his mouth is moving, but I can't hear shit.

I close my eyes and dip my head until my nose rests against the top of Nina's head. What he's saying doesn't matter right now. I finally, fucking *finally*, have our girl in my arms. She's safe and alive; that's all that matters.

"Baby, give her here, please." I'm so lost in the feel of her against me that when Kai's begging voice registers, I startle. Blinking my eyes open feels like a chore, but my fiancé's talking to me. "Hey handsome, there you are."

I blink again and realize my back is against a wall. Frowning, I look around and that's when I notice it's not a wall. Trevor is wrapped around both of us.

"You looked wobbly," Kai explains softly, "and Trev needed to touch her so..."

Two birds with one stone. I nod and wiggle, my left leg rapidly falling asleep. "How long—"

"Only about a minute. You all kinda zoned out," Meg murmurs as Kai rubs a piece of Nina's hair between his fingers.

Will steps forward and kneels at my side. "I'll carry her to the couch." My grip on Nina tightens, and he narrows his eyes. "Henry, there's a high probability that when she wakes up, she'll freak out. Remember what I said? Touch is hard for her unless it's from her mom."

Swallowing the lump in my throat, I relax only because I feel Trevor's arms fall away from us. I follow his lead and help transfer Nina into her dad's arms. A tear slips free from my watering eyes as her warmth is taken from me.

"Up you go." Kai's voice in my ear is accompanied by a soft grunt as I'm pulled to my feet and ushered to the couch. My attention immediately snaps to Nina where she rests peacefully a cushion away. I want to reach out and touch her so damn bad I can't help but continue to cry softly.

I can't believe she's here. There were so many moments when I feared I would never see her again. And just moments ago, I had her in my arms.

Chapter 15

Nina

Fire races across my knees, rousing me with pain. It's definitely not the first time I've woken to stinging wounds. I'm used to it.

I refrain from opening my eyes so I can figure out what's going on without alerting anyone to my presence. Something warm rubs my knee, making me twitch, but it isn't me who hisses and lets out a curse.

"Ow, Kai!"

A throaty chuckle sends tingles down my spine, and I'm not sure if it's a good kind. I don't even know what a good tingle would be anymore, I guess. At least not any I would admit to.

"Sit still, baby."

My heart jolts. *Baby? Are they—*

"You're together?" That's my dad.

"Yes, sir." Henry—his voice is scratchy. "Kai proposed almost a year ago."

My mom and dad congratulate them.

I feel my soul crack down the middle, along with my biggest dream of all. Of course I noticed how Kai and Henry were with each other in high school, but I guess I just thought I could have them all. I was selfish to assume all four of them could see me as more than a friend.

I'm happy for them. *So happy,* I chant over and over again until resignation sets in. The sinking sensation that I lost them to each other turns into relief. I lost our potential love the day I was kidnapped. I'll just be grateful they have each other because there's no way anyone would want me.

I can't help but wonder if they were relieved. Did they immediately jump into their relationship when I went missing? Was I just in the way? We were all building something; *I know it,* but maybe they wished for a different outcome. *Looks like they got it.*

My dad yanks me out of my self-deprecating thoughts with another topic that makes me want to break down and sob. "If you're going to stick around, there are a few other things you should know."

"Will," Mom snaps, and the rubbing on my knee stops. "Not when Nina's—"

Pulling on all the numbness I have in my arsenal, I let a slight disassociation settle over me like a heavy blanket. "It's fine, Mom," I whisper while peeling my eyes open.

She gasps and leans over me so she's all I can see. "Are you okay, sweetheart? You collapsed!"

I nod and apologize softly. She helps pull me into a sitting position and tucks a blanket over me. Ignoring all the eyes on me, I shift my butt back into the corner and pull my legs into my chest. I feel nothing as the small wounds on my knees pull.

My shields are up. The four male voices saying things to me go unheard.

"Go ahead, Dad." I cut the guys off and drop my head onto my legs. Seeing their pitying looks is the last thing I need right now. We all know this won't work and once Dad gives them a little slice of my issues, they'll be out the door so fast.

Gosh, I was so stupid to reach for Henry. If he knew even a fraction of who I am now and what my body looks like, he would have shied away from me.

"Best we get this over with," I all but whimper into the darkness of my folded frame.

Even with my intentional avoidance, I recognize Trevor's voice. "I don't think this is a good idea." *Perfect, he gets it!* "I'd rather hear from you, Neen, when you're ready."

That's not....that's not going to happen. "Mom..." I peek at her.

The understanding in her gaze helps relax me and when she acknowledges my nod to continue, the battle to keep my eyes dry begins. Dad sucks in a breath and I know what he says will feel like opening wounds that have barely healed. But he would do anything for me and so he explains some of my deepest traumas.

"Nina escaped. We still aren't sure how long she ran through those woods for. By the time the police found the cabin she was kept at, it was nothing but ash in the middle of absolute nowhere."

Monster. Mr. M.

"Breathe, sweetie." Mom's reminder to continue living inflates my lungs.

"When she came to the hospital..." Dad clears his throat. "Nina wasn't in a mental state to come home. The doctors were worried about..."

He can't say it. "Suicide," I blurt harshly and squeeze my eyes shut. Tears tickle my cheeks. *Why are they still here?*

The pained grunts that go around the room make me want to run away from the conversation. Before anyone can ask what I'm sure they're dying to know, I uncurl from my blanket and quickly walk around the couch, away from the rising tension. My breaths are labored as I climb the stairs.

"She was in the psych facility for a year before they deemed her safe to come home." My mom's broken voice digs the hole and my dad's words nail the coffin. "We're still scared."

I hear nothing else as I close the door to my bedroom. I flip the lock, not caring what happens downstairs any longer. All this time and nothing I've done has made my parents happy. It's a good thing I moved out.

If I'm alone, there's nobody to disappoint.

Chapter 16

Trevor

*S*uicide. Suicide. That's what Nina said. That's what her doctors were worried about. What her parents are *still* terrified of. Would she do it? End her life?

There's still so much I don't know and it's eating me alive. *How the hell am I supposed to be there for her if I have no clue what she needs? Has she eaten breakfast?* It was way past dinnertime when she ran from us, and the pizza hadn't been touched.

Will and Meg asked us to leave shortly after we heard Nina lock her bedroom door upstairs. It may as well have been a fucking gunshot going off for how much it killed me to be shut out from my girl. And she *is* my girl. I know she's convinced we'll run once we know more about what she suffered, but it did the complete opposite.

My instincts are driving me to run to her and never leave her side. I have to remind Nina who we are and the bond we used to share as children. *The guys will agree with me that—*

"Sit the fuck down, dude."

Irritation flares, making my back itch with prickling sweat.

"Fuck off, Ridge." He sighs but otherwise returns to watching his show.

We haven't seen Nina in almost sixteen hours. How the hell am I supposed to relax? I have no fucking clue what's going on with my cousin, but whatever it is, it's about to whip him upside the goddamn face.

"Get your shoes on. We're leaving," I declare, snatching my wallet and keys off the kitchen island. Owning a line of resorts gives us badass privileges, like staying in a room that's more like a decent sized apartment. Kai and Henry are next door, so I'll just message them the plan.

Plan infiltrate Nina's life like we never left has been initiated.

I almost forget I told Ridge to get ready, then he opens his broody mouth. "No thanks." Slumped on the couch, I can almost imagine him as a pouting teenager. Now that I think about it, he did this a lot in middle school and high school.

"I'm not asking." I throw one of his tennis shoes at him and feel sick satisfaction when it thumps him hard in the thigh. Tuning out his grumbled protests, I wait by the door as I try to rein in my impatience.

Ridge has always struggled more than me, Kai, and Henry. We've all had our bouts of depression, but when Ridge sinks, he drowns. He'll never admit it, but he's sensitive and feels *hard*.

On the drive to Nina's, I sneak peeks at my cousin. Growing up the way we did with absent parents that traded childcare means we grew up far closer than some siblings. The part-time nanny at my place was always stoned out by the pool, and Ridge's nanny spent more time snooping in the mansion than anything else. We only had each other and Kai.

Kai introduced Henry to us in middle school after Henry helped him with some schoolwork. I'll never forget the look on Henry's face when he laid eyes on Nina for the first time. He was stunned speechless, but weren't we all? Which was the exact reason Ridge was practically begging her to eat with us that day in the cafeteria.

"Why are we going back there, Trev? Will said not to."

Grinding my jaw, I fight the urge to shove him. Since I'm driving, I pack my words with a punch instead. "You aren't fooling anyone, Ridge. The guilt isn't only yours to hold. You can't take that shit away from us. Acting like you're the reason, the *only* reason, Nina was kidnapped and tortured for two years is completely invalidating to the rest of us."

I feel the weight of his glare before he asks, "The fuck are you on about? It *is* my fault. *I* should have brought her home. *I* let her walk out of my house without a second thought. And *I* changed my number. If it weren't for me, she would have years of happiness instead of bruises and suicidal thoughts! If I hadn't changed my number, we would have known she was safe and *alive* years ago!"

His shouting doesn't faze me. It's a fairly normal occurrence when he gets into a rut. If it weren't for me and my dominant tendencies, he would have thrown himself off the deep end a long time ago. He has a close relationship with self-sabotage.

"Who told you to cut ties with our families, Ridge?"

"What?" he snaps, breathing hard. I repeat my question only for him to scoff off my meaning. "You didn't make me do shit, Trevor. The choice was all mine."

Thankfully, just as my temper gets the best of me, I pull into Nina's driveway and throw the truck into park. A big sigh puffs from my lips as I scrub my hand down my face, but when that does nothing to alleviate my rage at Ridge or myself, I slam my hand into the steering wheel.

"The fuck?!"

"Shut *up*, Ridge. For just a damn second." Breathing heavily, I try to rein in my control as my emotions continue to slip. "You wanna play the guilty game? Fine. Here you go."

I turn in my seat and look my cousin dead in the eye. "Will asked Nina to come home earlier that day to help set something up for her party. Kai and Henry were supposed to pick her up after the movie they went to see at the theater, so they didn't get her text until it was too late. Nina chose to walk home, thinking there was no harm in an easy twenty-minute stroll in the summer across town. You didn't think twice about letting her walk out the door."

"I would have brought her home. I was so wrapped up in my new painting," he whispers brokenly, staring straight ahead like he can remember that day as vividly as if it were yesterday. "I should have—"

"Nina didn't tell you she was walking home when she left you in your art room." My tone leaves no room for argument. I'm stating facts. "Meg didn't even know what Nina was up to that day since she was so focused on the sweet sixteen party. I was lazing around at home that day."

Fast forward to the day we told our families to fuck off. "*And* I'm the one who shattered your phone, brought you to the store the next day, then set both of us up on a new plan with new numbers. Me. I made the decision to cut us off from our family. Meg could have easily called me instead of you and gotten the same result."

I swallow, hating everything about all of it. "Don't you see? We all hold some responsibility for what happened. Meg, Will, *Nina*, Henry, Kai, you, me. Don't hold all of our actions on your own. Had one of us done something different, everything could have been better."

I've never said all of that out loud, but he needed to hear it. Hell, *I* needed to hear it. Ridge sits there silently staring off into space. Instead of demanding a response, I unbuckle his seatbelt and mine. "Come on," I mumble and hop out of the truck.

He has a lot to think about and facts to sort through, but he can do that on Nina's couch while I make sure she's eaten something. Hearing the door slam behind me has me relaxing a little, knowing I don't have to drag Ridge into Nina's home.

We all just need a little Neen to heal our worried hearts.

Chapter 17

Nina

I've been staring out my living room window for a long time now. I wish I could say I was relaxing and watching the day pass, but I'm not. This is purely another show of my anxiety.

Living at my parents' house helped me feel secure, knowing I always had them there to keep me safe. I could lock myself in my room all day without feeling like I needed to keep watch around the house.

Here, I'm alone. My dad isn't my shield any longer. There's nobody to keep me safe but myself.

Mr. M is still out there and even if evidence points to him being near the Canadian border recently, I won't feel safe until he's no longer walking the earth. My safety relies on a monster's demise. I've long since given up wondering if that makes me a terrible person.

My neck pops as I shift on the recliner. With a groan, I close my eyes and stretch the stiff muscles that are giving me a headache. The burning sensation in my eyes makes me wonder how long I've been keeping watch. Instead of resting them, I blink a few times to focus back on my task.

Once locked back in, that's when I see them. Trevor and Ridge sitting in a truck in my driveway. *I close my eyes for one dang second...*This just reiterates the need to stay vigilant.

Through their windshield I watch as Trevor flails his arms and I have half a moment of curiosity before it fades away into a whisper of what could have been. I'm snapped out of my thoughts when Trevor opens his door.

Immediately, my heart lodges itself in my throat and I bolt for my bedroom upstairs. Each slam of my bare feet on the hardwoods matches the thundering in my chest. Flying into my bedroom, I lunge for my dresser and quickly swap my shorts for leggings. My tank top is quickly covered with a sweatshirt in my closet and before I can think of what else I need to cover, the doorbell rings.

"Oh God," I whisper frantically, turning in a circle in hopes that my spotless bedroom will give me advice. *What else, what else...what am I missing?* My sweaty foot slides a little on the floorboards, giving me the exact reminder that I needed.

A soft knock downstairs jolts me into action. With a ball of socks in my hand, I sit on my bed and shamefully cover the smattering of scars on the soles of my feet. *Yes, I'm so scarred and hideous that I can't even show my feet.*

Another knock. *Dang persistent men...*

As light as I can possibly manage, I leave my room and tiptoe down the stairs. If they happen to be walking away, I'd prefer not to alert them to me being close. *No such luck.*

"Neen?" I close my eyes as agony rips through me. "You in there?" Trevor calls through my front door.

"Trev, maybe we should—"

"Shut up, Ridge. She's home, and I'll wait her out for as long as it takes."

I sigh, knowing Trevor won't give up until he at least accomplished what he came here for. With my next inhale, I imagine all my protective layers settling into place. Some might imagine my shoulders going back and my chin rising in mock confidence, but I actually do the opposite.

With my hair tumbled forward shielding my face and my shoulders slouched forward to make me seem smaller, I unlock the door, then open it an inch.

I don't say a word, waiting for Trev to see that I am still alive and get him out of here fast. Obviously I knew he wouldn't just look at me and leave, but when he breathes my name, I startle before taking a step back.

"Nina..." Trevor whispers and steps toward me. I walk backward, scared, not necessarily of him, but of the way my numbness is rapidly disintegrating and forcing my feelings to the surface. "Say something. *Please?*"

The way my belly swoops and my eyes burn when I glance up at him doesn't surprise me; it's why I tried to go numb. I should have known I would be powerless to ignore the full force of these men.

"H-hi," I whimper, stepping back again as Trevor enters my home followed by Ridge, who's cursing under his breath while closing my door.

"Shit, baby girl," Trevor croaks. "I've missed you."

Logically, I think I knew that, but it doesn't matter. They grieved the girl they knew, and she's gone. Despite the warning bells going off in my head, I mutter, "You miss a ghost."

"I don't believe that for one goddamn second," Trevor declares in a scarily rough tone. I shrug. What else is there to do? We disagree. "Have you eaten today?"

Knowing I can't force them out of my house, I turn around and make my way to the couch. Soon they'll get bored and leave.

"Nina. Did you eat?" I glance at Trevor and wiggle my head in a *so-so* gesture. "So that's a no," he huffs and stomps to my fridge.

Turning back around, not wanting to see him frown at my ridiculously full fridge, I kick my blanket away and curl up on my side. I'm aware that my behavior shows that I trust them in my home, but that's not all there is to it.

First of all, I'm exhausted. Tomorrow is my fourth day all on my own, and I couldn't be more lonely. Even if I rarely spoke much with my parents, I never felt so trapped in my own head. The noises Trevor makes in the kitchen helps to drown out the voices in my head.

Secondly, Ridge and Trev won't leave until they're ready. They were always bossy when we were growing up, and Trev was more overbearing. Although, as Ridge slumps down across from me in my abandoned recliner by the window, I imagine it wouldn't be hard to get him to go away. He looks ready to bolt at any moment. Actually, he looks super angry.

The edge of panic I was riding on when they pulled in seems a lot closer now that I'm studying the hard frown behind his glasses. Staring at my legs, he looks ready to attack me like—

I sniffle, and it's then I realize tears are streaming down my face and onto my pillow. Never mind the numb layers, they're all but gone, having disintegrated in the face of Ridge's obvious discomfort.

He doesn't want to be here. Why would he? I'm broken and utterly unwell.

I swallow and it must be loud, because Ridge snaps his eyes to mine. Mustering up any courage I can find, I give him the out I'm sure he needs to flee without guilt. "You can go," I whisper and tuck my hand under my head.

His frown only deepens, so I squeeze my eyelids shut and

beg silently for him to go away. If all they'll do is bring me pain, then I don't want them here.

"I would never hurt you, Nina."

A sob rips through my throat, shattering my final flimsy barrier of numbness.

Chapter 18

Ridge

What have I done?

"Shit! What happened?!" *When the hell did Kai and Henry get here?* "Ridge, what happened?" Kai demands, skidding to his knees in front of Nina.

"I-I don't know," I stutter out, feeling shell-shocked. My first words to her make her break down into sobs. What does that say about me?

"Hey." Henry comes over to me after dropping a few bags on the kitchen table. "Walk me through it?"

Trevor comes barreling over, and I watch as he knocks Kai's hand away from Nina. Muttering back and forth, Kai finally leans back and gives her some space. "Baby, can you look at me, please?" Trev asks her, his voice like gravel.

"Sh-she told me I could go, then she was whispering about us hurting her. I told her I would never hurt her, and this happened." I wave my arm at Nina who's now quietly sniffling into her hands. Henry nods thoughtfully with a sad look on his face.

When Nina chokes a little, Trevor's spine straightens. In a tone I've never heard before, he demands her attention. "Nina, look at me. Now."

My throat clogs when she opens her eyes and peeks at my cousin between her fingers. She looks so small. So fragile. Nothing like the young girl who used to whip my ass in any sport.

"Good girl."

My eyebrows rise to my hairline when Nina visibly relaxes at his praise. *Interesting.*

Trevor keeps talking. "There you go. Just breathe, Neen. I don't want you getting worked up again after choking like that."

I'm envious of the way she hangs on to his every word. Hell, I say one sentence and it upsets her. Trevor seems like a fucking God at this moment. *Maybe I need to pull out some Dom shit to get her to feel comfortable with me again.*

With me across from her in a recliner, Henry standing by me, Kai sitting on the ground by her feet, and Trevor crouched beside her, I'm shocked we aren't scaring her. *Already did that, dipshit.* She moves her hands and wipes her tears away as she pushes into a sitting position.

"Good. Good job," Trevor murmurs, reaching to brush a stray hair off her face. *That* is something I wouldn't have done. I'm proven right not a beat later when she squeaks and presses into the cushions behind her. "Shit. I'm sorry, Nina."

Her eyes which were relaxed until Trevor tried to touch her now ping-pong between the four of us. Realizing she's surrounded, her breathing picks up.

Keeping my volume low, I suggest, "Maybe we should go."

Nina sniffs, and Trevor shoots a glare over his shoulder at me. "We aren't leaving."

Henry shifts beside me, seemingly uncomfortable, but my

irritation flares. "Are you blind? We're making her uncomfortable. This isn't helping."

"Are we making you uncomfortable?" Kai asks Nina, looking like he's being tortured. She glances at him but doesn't say anything. I sigh and her lip wobbles.

She pulls her knees up to her chest. A tear slips down her cheek and her gaze moves to her lap. "Y-you can go."

That's exactly what she said to me five fucking minutes ago. Why the hell does she keep saying that? I wish she would just tell me what she wants.

Trevor's hands clench like he's fighting the urge to touch her, then the oven timer beeps. With a curse, he stands, mumbling about not wanting the nachos to burn.

Henry moves to sit on the coffee table in front of her. He glances at me, then at Nina. That goes on a few times, like he's pondering something. Finally, he shares with the class. "Neen. Do you think we don't want to be here?"

Something about Henry talking or him being near helps her shoulders relax from her ears. She nods and looks at him. My heart cracks at the pleading look in her eyes. *What does she need? And more importantly, why can't she just tell us?* The Nina we all knew had zero issues expressing herself. This is infuriating because it leaves way too much unspoken, which I swear to hell is what my anxiety feeds on.

"What makes you think that?" Henry's approach to hold a curious edge seems to coax Nina out of her shell.

Trevor comes back with a plate of nachos and takes a seat a few feet away from Nina on the couch. She eyes him warily and scrunches her nose at the plate of food. *She used to love nachos.*

"We'll get to that look soon, baby. But first," Trevor nods his head, "answer Henry."

Nina gulps, and when her attention flicks to me, I feel a

sense of dread. *I'm the problem.* "Ridge...Ridge isn't happy. You all should go."

"I don't want to go," I blurt. *I won't fucking leave her side if she keeps talking to us!*

"But you—" She goes white as a sheet and gulps.

Fear. What is she afraid of?

"It's okay, Nina," Henry coos and brings his legs up onto the coffee table to sit crisscrossed. "No matter what you say, we won't hurt you. Or be mad at you."

I don't know if she believes him, but his words help me understand a bit more of what's going on. Nina's afraid of confrontation. How deep does that conditioning run?

Since I've already upset her enough for the day, I let her off the hook. "I'm sorry, Nina girl. I came in here with a lot on my mind and I know I didn't carry that well. I *do* want to be here."

Nina watches me for a moment before nodding softly. When Kai asks her if she wants us to go, she only shrugs and tugs on the string of her blanket. *Anxiety?*

"Well," Trev cuts in. "We aren't going anywhere until you eat a bite of your lunch."

By the look on her face, we might never leave.

Chapter 19

Nina

They did *not* leave. In fact, they stayed for a few more hours.

I'm still contemplating the weirdness of yesterday, making it hard for me to continue reading. I had a few bites of the nachos before I felt like I was going to be sick. Making them feel welcome in my house was asking way too much when they just barged in. But I didn't need to do anything for them to make themselves at home.

Henry migrated to the ground beside his fiancé, Trevor stayed on the couch near me, and Ridge kept his place in the recliner. For hours, all they did was talk to each other. I must not have said more than a few words, but it didn't matter. Conversation ebbed and flowed naturally.

I tried so hard to keep my eyes trained on the TV, yet I couldn't keep myself from stealing glances. So many times I wondered just what the heck they were doing hanging out in my living room. Aside from the occasional bathroom breaks, random phone calls, and trips to my kitchen for snacks, they stayed in the living room with me until I started yawning.

Something about having so many people interacting around me took all my energy. Or maybe it was the ever present thrum of anxiety. Ridge was right. They did make me uncomfortable; the whole time, honestly. But there was a security in having them here. Similar to when I'm in a room with my dad, my mind gets all fuzzy like it's taking a rest.

Huffing, I flip the cover on my e-reader and debate getting out of bed. Life is easier in the confines of my blankets. Until the doorbell rings and I have to contemplate my choices.

Ding-Dong!

Nibbling on the inside of my cheek, I tap the screen on my phone and see it's midafternoon. *Sheesh, I've been stuck in my book for a few hours.* My bladder screams, effectively urging me out of bed.

As I'm wiggling out of my sheets, the doorbell rings again. Grumbling, I fly out of my room and down the stairs. "Nina?" Kai hollers, setting me at ease.

Now knowing who's here, I unlock the door and fling it open before hightailing my butt to the bathroom.

"Are you okay?" *So Henry's here too.*

"Pee!" I basically screech and slam the bathroom door behind me with a *boom* that makes me jump. Once my bladder's empty, a blush heats my face and neck. *Oh my God...Who screams* pee *like that?*

Sweat beads on my lower back as I realize I need to go back out there and face them. *How embarrassing.* Why they haven't run for the hills, I'll never know. I wish I would have paid more attention to their conversations yesterday instead of zoning out and letting my mind shut off.

I can't do that again. I may have known them as boys, but I don't know them as men. Although Mom and Dad wouldn't have told them about me if they thought the guys were dangerous.

They *are* dangerous though. I'm terrified of the way they infiltrated my life yesterday. It seemed so easy for them to take up space and quiet my demons.

Yeah, they're dangerous. I can't let them in like that anymore because the look on Kai's face when I saw him watching my meltdown about near killed me. My emotions hurt him, and when I saw the sadness and confusion flicker in Ridge's eyes, my heart cracked right down the middle.

They may never inflict harm on me, but I'm damaged. I'll shred them just as Mr. M shredded me. They won't have the brutal scars I do; the wounds would be beneath the surface. If I allow them in, I'm dooming us all.

I've had enough pain in my life. I can't stand any more hits.

Having Kai, Henry, Trevor and Ridge here again has me closer to keeling over in agony. They are a reminder of all that I used to be. Every time I spoke a word yesterday, I watched hope flare in their eyes.

Soon they will learn there's no hope for this broken thing.

Chapter 20

Kai

My laughter dies a slow death the longer Nina doesn't come out of the bathroom. It's been almost ten minutes. The first seven, I figured she needed to do other stuff in there, but now I'm not so sure.

"Should I go check on her?" Ridge murmurs, looking uncomfortable at the idea of disrupting her privacy. Like we aren't disrupting it by showing up unannounced two days in a row.

"I'll do it," I say and only hesitate for a second before I'm walking down the hall. I tap two knuckles softly on the bathroom door so as not to scare her. "Nina?"

Nothing.

Glancing back toward the other three, Trevor looks ready to kick the door down. I hold up a finger in hopes of taming the beast. Henry might have been better for this job, but I need her to know I'm here and she can count on me too.

"Are you okay in there?" I call out again. No answer.

I wanted to chase her when she ran to the bathroom in her

big sweatshirt and bare legs on display. Now, I really fucking wish I would have. Hoping the door is unlocked, I grab the handle.

"I'm coming in." The knob turns and with a small push, it opens, shocking the shit out of me. "Neen?"

Fuck, I hate pushing her boundaries, but why the hell isn't she responding?

The first thing I notice when I step into the bathroom is the scent of roses. Breathing in like an addict, my energy boosts. Then I find Nina with her hands on the countertop and her head hung.

"Flora?" My voice is thick with worry, and when the nickname I gave her when we were kids slips out, I almost cry. *What I wouldn't give for her to call me—*

"Fauna..." Nina's reply is nothing but a puff of air and still it blows me away.

"I-I missed that." What a lame thing to say. "I missed *you*." I don't get a verbal response, but her body seems to droop even more. "What are you doing in here? I was getting worried."

"That's the problem." Shocked by yet another statement from her, I blink with my mouth hanging open. She continues. "I don't want you to worry."

A humorless laugh escapes me. "That's all we've ever done when it comes to you. I remember worrying about you from the moment I met you. Hell, every time I pitched you a baseball, I was terrified I would hit you. Or, Christ, you could have lost your balance and stubbed your toe at any given second."

I let my eyes scan her from head to toe. What I don't expect to see is a wicked scar on her calf. My entire body tenses and my jaw cracks. *What the fuck happened there?!* It looks like something took a chunk out of her leg.

Nina's tiny voice breaks me out of my murderous stare down with her leg. "This is different."

If my tone drops a few octaves, it's because I'm fucking pissed. "No, Nina. It's just stronger now. I've always worried about you and I always will. You're the flora to my fauna."

She sighs and turns around. I try not to react to the obvious exhaustion on her face, but I can't resist stepping forward. "Why are you guys here, Kai?"

I frown. "Why wouldn't we be here?"

Dropping her eyes, she shakes her head. "I don't know what you want from me. I have nothing to give."

"That's not true," I state adamantly, wishing like hell I could hug her. Just the fact that she's holding a conversation with me has my heart pounding. Is she more comfortable with only one of us at a time? That's not going to work well. Henry, Trev, Ridge and I are a package deal. Nina too. We just have to prove it to her.

"Come on." I add some cheer to my tone and back out of the bathroom. "I'll show you what we want from you."

Eyeing me like I could be a predator, she side steps me and exits. I watch in satisfaction as she blushes up at Henry when she realizes he was right outside the bathroom the whole time.

"Hi, pretty girl," my fiancé greets her with a soft smile.

"Hi," she whispers while shifting on her bare feet and wringing her hands together.

Henry's smile widens and instead of heeding any of the warnings we've received, he reaches out, then takes hold of one of her hands. She gasps. Hell, *I* fucking gasp and gape at them as she allows him to lead her toward the kitchen.

"Here," he beams and guides her to a stool at the island. "Trev's making grilled cheese with ham and seasoned fries. I brought tartar sauce."

Like a deer in the headlights, Nina blinks at him.

Then Trevor swoops in with a fry. "Open, baby." She does without a second thought. "Crispy enough?"

I swear I see a happy little smile ghosting over her lips when she nods. Maybe, just *maybe,* we can be what she needs.

Chapter 21

Nina

"**W**hy are you blushing?"

"Nina?"

Someone clears their throat, annoying me. "What?" I mumble, still attempting to read through the distractions.

"Pretty girl."

A finger tickling my cheek makes me suck in a breath, just like the girl in my book. Henry smirks at my reaction, but he can't possibly know the low thrum coursing through my body right now. That one little touch while reading *that* has my mouth filling with saliva.

Kai went upstairs to get my eReader when I was bored. I've been lost in my own world ever since. Considering the way my ass hurts, I doubt I've moved for a few hours.

It's not Henry who says something about my reaction, though. Kai reaches for my e-reader from behind me. "Please put me out of my misery and tell me what the hell you're reading that has you wiggling and blushing like that?"

I scramble to keep hold of my device. "I—"

A cold French fry enters my line of sight. "Open," Trevor demands. I scrunch my nose but do as he asks.

"No more," I say while chewing, but that leaves my attention split, thus allowing Ridge to snatch my book from my hands. Screeching, I try to lunge for him, but he's securely on the other side of my coffee table now.

"*If you're about to come all over my leg, you'll use my first fucking name, Miss Sessions,*" Ridge reads, and I swear I beg anything listening to let the ground swallow me whole. "Damn, Neen. You're a little kinky, huh?" he teases.

I'm so mortified and trying to think of the best way to make him stop when a cold sensation tickles the back of my leg. I didn't think this moment could get any worse. Honestly, I'd rather Ridge keep reading my smut.

When they got here a few hours ago, I was running for the bathroom in my shorts. I know Kai saw one of my most brutal scars, but I completely forgot about it until this moment.

These guys are just so...so...*overwhelming.* I don't have time to think around them. They take so much space inside my head that everything goes quiet. This morning I struggled to pay attention to my book, but with them buzzing around my house, encouraging me to continue eating my lunch in small portions and playing cards at my dining room table, I was able to let everything go.

Sure, I still glanced out my front window from time to time to make sure Mr. M wasn't here, but I think my heart, mind, body, and soul finally took a much needed break.

I'm not sure why they want to be here, but I don't have the confidence to ask or to kick them out. And why would I? In a shocking turn of events, I think I like having them here. I have to remind myself it's only day two of seeing them again.

Pressure on my calf makes me stiffen. Then Trevor growls

out a question that makes my eyes immediately fill with tears. "What is this?"

Knowledge equals pain. And I really don't want to cause even a fraction of the pain I suffered.

"You-you should go." *Push them away. Push. Push! PUSH!* "I-I don't w-want you here."

"Bullshit. I call bullshit, Nina." Ridge sounds angry. He throws my e-reader down on the recliner and pins me with a look that forces a tear down my cheek. "What is Trevor looking at?"

Trembling, I wrap my arms around my waist and try to gather my strength. "S-stop touching me." *I want my mom.*

"Trev," Henry murmurs. "Move away. Now."

Trevor's fingers disappear and somehow my leg feels colder without his touch.

Still, I don't look behind me. I can't bear to see the looks on their faces. Kai's seen it, but after Henry had me sit on the stool, I managed to sneak away to the couch without them noticing. Ridge stealing my e-reader was the catalyst for this moment. In desperation to keep him from embarrassing me like when we were kids, I stood from the couch, dropping my blanket and leaving my scar on full display. All Trevor had to do was look down.

Of course he looked down. *Why did he have to look down?*

Ridge's jaw ticks before he stomps around the side of the couch. A whimper slips free when I hear him curse.

"Guys stop." Henry's standing and grabbing my bicep before I can run away from him. A startled gasp explodes from me when a rush of warm air chases away my chills. "There you go. Deep breaths."

Once I have my breathing under control, I just stare at Henry. He brought me outside. *How did I not notice walking outside?* My back patio is my most favorite part of my house with its twinkly lights, grill—not that I know how to use it—and the fire-pit. The outdoor furniture surrounding the brick circle looks perfectly comfy too.

Black curls in disarray, Henry looks calm considering what just happened. Each new piece of information coming to light brings them closer to running for the hills. I decide I have to tell them things when they ask. They deserve to know how messed up I am.

So I give Henry a broken piece of me. "His dog." I shudder and curl up on the outdoor sofa. "When I ran away."

Afraid to find that I was right, I don't look at him. I'm disgusting and broken. I'm missing a chunk of my calf. So much of my blood is in the tangled web of woods in Colorado.

Who *wants* to risk picking up shattered pieces of glass? Because that's what I am. There's no hope of repairing my broken pieces. And there's only so many times someone can ignore broken glass before it's swept and thrown away.

If Henry says anything, I don't hear it. The memories I've fought so hard to ignore can no longer be battled by their presence. Trevor shoved me below the surface with his questions. Ridge took away my floaties when he vocalized his displeasure of my leg. And Henry offered a life raft.

But do I want to be saved?

Chapter 22

Henry

Two steps forward, ten steps back. I knew our luck was going to run out at some point, but goddamn it Trevor. Sometimes he has no tact and *sometimes* that works in his favor. Like his obvious Dom shit that he was pulling to get her to eat. It was helpful that she was distracted by her book which we can thank Kai for.

He didn't even have to say anything. Just plopped the e-reader in her lap and sat beside her. Our girl didn't hesitate to flip the cover open and escape the world for a few hours.

It was nice, just being in her presence. As much as we really fucking wanted to talk to her, it was amazing to be near her. Maybe this way is for the best. The more we're around, the faster it will be for her to get used to us.

I know we won't ever go back to how we used to be, and I would be lying if I said that didn't give me immense sadness, but this can be a beautiful new beginning. *If* and only *if* we learn her triggers fast.

Trevor, while I love him and can appreciate his take charge

action, should not have touched her scar. Hell, he shouldn't have even asked about it. It was obvious her emotions were already running high with Ridge messing around.

"Hi, honey."

"Christ!" I hiss and smudge nail polish all down the side on Nina's middle toe.

Meg giggles and crouches in front of Nina. "Sorry, Henry. Didn't mean to scare you." I tell her it's alright, but her attention is already fixed on her daughter. "She's so tired."

Shortly after Nina curled up on the couch outside, she dozed off. I'm not sure what that says about me, but the fact that she felt secure enough gives me hope.

"She feels safe with you," Meg murmurs, flicking her gaze up to me and down to Nina's feet in my lap. I give her a small smile and go back to painting Nina's toenails. "Did she tell you?"

I shake my head, focusing on making her pinky toe perfect. "No. She dozed off and Kai found some nail polish in the bathroom and brought it out." We're both silent for a moment, before I add, "Her nails never used to be bare."

Meg sniffles and rises before curling up in her own chair. She looks so small in the dark with the soft light of the gas fire showing her worn expression. "No, they never used to be," she says softly. "Many things aren't the same, Henry. That's why I didn't try to make contact again after the first attempt."

At that, I give her a hard look. "You should have tried again."

Meg shakes her head. "No, honey. Had you known, all four of you would have moved back home."

"Exactly. She needed us. We should have been there." I'm not one to get angry, especially not with such a delicate situation, but this is *Nina* we're talking about.

"The only thing Nina needed was to heal."

Forget the fucking nail polish. "We should have been there to help her heal, Meg. I love you, but—"

"Don't ever disrespect such wonderful vows with the word *but* young man." *Shit.* "You were so young. You still are. And that's why I have to explain this to you."

Explain what? Nothing will change my mind that I could have helped Nina when she needed me the most.

"You couldn't have helped her, Henry. Neither could the other three. Will and I couldn't either. Nina may have escaped, but she sure as heck didn't know if she wanted to survive. The girl we met in the hospital wasn't the same Nina we knew. Not even the Nina we know now."

Meg's openly crying, and it makes me feel like shit. *Where the hell is Will?* Just as I think his name, the patio door opens and Will walks out with the other three guys. "Henry," Nina's dad greets me.

Kissing the top of his daughter's head, he releases a breath of air that almost seems like relief. "She won't be asleep much longer."

"How do you know?" Trevor asks.

Will takes a seat beside his wife. "She only sleeps a few hours at a time. When she sleeps, she sleeps hard, though."

Capping the nail polish draws attention to what I had been doing. Trev freezes, and Ridge curses.

The bottoms of Nina's feet have one white puckered scar after another. There are too many questions, too many worries to ask just one.

A subtle jolt and stiffening from Nina gives me pause. *Is she awake?* Glancing at her so as not to alert anyone else, I catch her squint at the fire just as her foot twitches. Rubbing my finger along her ankle to soothe her stops her from yanking away from me. Nina looks at me and the most beautiful thing happens. She relaxes and closes her eyes.

I give her ankle a small squeeze. *Thank you for trusting me. I won't tell them you're awake.*

Thankfully, Meg continues our previous conversation. "Nina needed to *want* help before she could accept it. That's what I was getting at Henry. Even just Will and I there at the hospital with her was an immense bout of pressure."

Kai frowns at Nina's parents as he sits on the arm of the couch beside me. "What do you mean?"

"Nina's default is to push people away. It's taken a lot of therapy for her to overcome some of that, but she's finally been in a place where she asks us, mainly Meg, when she needs something. Our sweet girl is a closed book."

Will's explanation gives me pause. Stealing a glance at Nina, my heart breaks when I see a tear slip from her eyelashes. "But she seems close with you both still." My words come out sounding like a question, and I guess they are. I'm confused. Nina always loved her parents growing up.

Meg gives me another sad smile. "That took years, honey. And while my relationship with her might look similar, her trust in Will is still a work in progress." Meg's words make Will flinch. "While she is wary of anyone, it was a *man* who h-hurt her. If you're here to stay—" Nina twitches, and I grip her legs firmly. "—then you need to be prepared for the long haul."

We're all silent, watching the flames dance. Until Will breaks it, and my heart. "That's enough for tonight. Time you boys got some rest. We'll stay with Nina for a while."

Another foot twitch. *Come on, pretty girl, tell me what you want. Tell me to stay.*

"Come on, baby," Kai says, kissing the top of my head. Nina stiffens again, but maybe it's just because I'm moving her legs.

Ignoring Will's warning, I lean over my girl and whisper, "I'm prepared." I wipe away her tear and add, "See you tomorrow."

And the next day. And the next day. And the next until we're old and gray. Just like we always planned.

Chapter 23

Trevor

"So what's the plan?"

I could strangle my cousin. "What do you mean, what's the plan?"

Upside down on the couch with his legs in the air, Ridge narrows his eyes at me. "When are we going home? We have work to do. We can't stay here forever."

So much rage builds up I can't control the acid dripping from my tone. "As far as I'm fucking concerned, our home is with Nina." *How dare he suggest anything else is important?*

His glare turns into a confused frown as he sits up, jostling Henry at the same time. "Trev, I'm just saying we have a company to run. People are counting on us."

I open my mouth to snap back like I've been doing with him a lot the past few days, but Henry cuts me off. "Ridge is right."

The asshat who is supposedly *right* waves a hand at our friend in a *see?* motion. "I'm not suggesting we just leave Nina and forget about her, man. We need to think about our other priorities."

I don't *want* other priorities.

Kai adds, "If we're moving here—"

"Woah, what?!" Ridge shouts. "We haven't talked about moving!"

With a deadpan stare, Kai asks the million dollar question. "Do you not want to move, Ridge? Because I'm going to be honest, Henry and I would like to be closer to Nina. She's the heart of our group, always has been, and we don't want to be without our girl."

Ridge stays quiet, and I don't say anything either. Obviously I plan on moving here, hell I'd love to move in with Nina and make sure she's cared for, but that's about a million steps away. I suppose I could force the issue. *Maybe I can get Meg in on it with me and—*

"What if..." Ridge trails off, staring into his lap like his sweatpants have all the answers. Henry nudges his arm in encouragement. "What if Neen doesn't want us here?"

"She does," I say without hesitation. "And before you ask, I know because her dad hasn't kicked us to the curb."

Kai looks thoughtful. "You think she would tell her parents if we made her uncomfortable?"

Henry nods and agrees with me. "Without a doubt."

"It's just going to take time to get her to open up. And I think her letting us in is going to look different for each of us." Pacing around the hotel suite living room, I think through our couple days of interactions so far.

"When did you become so wise?" Ridge grumbles.

Ignoring him, I continue. "We need to go about this the right way." A lightbulb goes off in my head. "And she's already shown us."

Ridge chooses this moment to sass. "Care to share with the class? Then maybe we should have an actual discussion about uprooting our lives, yeah?"

Henry glares at Ridge this time, but everyone's attention

shifts back to me almost immediately. "I've been trying to watch how she is with each of us. Kai," I look to my friend, "Nina feels comfortable talking to you. Henry, you're the only one she doesn't flinch away from when you touch her."

Henry nods and twists his lips.

Kai points at me and snaps his fingers. "Yeah, I noticed that. Shocked the shit out of me. And she lets you boss her around," he says to me.

She does, and fuck if it doesn't make the alpha male in me roar with pleasure. *The things I would like to try...*

"And what about me?" Ridge interrupts my dirty thoughts. "All I seem to do is bother Nina or make her uncomfortable."

Henry takes this one. "You challenge her," he declares without much thought, and it's true.

Ridge is a pain in the ass, but pain evokes feeling, and that's exactly what he does for our Nina. When he pushes her buttons, she trades her worried avoidance or passive glance for a spitting glare, or literal tears that show he brought up some big emotion in her.

Surprisingly, my cousin doesn't deny it and watches the wall intently. After a few minutes of us all lost in our thoughts, he asks the question I knew was burning a hole in his brain. "So, are we moving here? To be...to be with Nina?"

Ridge looks so uncertain my heart cracks down the center for him. He's battling some self-worth shit that I have no clue how to help him with. I've already laid out where the blame lies, but it's going to take more than me to make him feel better. *He needs Nina.*

"Henry and I are," Kai replies slowly while both he and his fiancé study mine and Ridge's expressions. "We'd like for you both to come too, and get another place for all of us, but I know it's a lot to ask. We love you guys, but—"

Henry stiffens. "No. No *buts* should ever follow an *I love you* statement."

"We love you, and we love Nina," Kai amends with a little smirk at Henry who huffs and tries to hide a smile. "We want the five of us together again but—" He looks at Henry to see if he'll get scolded, when he doesn't Kai continues. "We understand if it's a commitment you aren't ready to make."

"Good job," Henry murmurs and kisses Kai on the cheek. The happy bastard beams and cuddles Henry into his side.

"I need a second," Ridge whispers and rushes from the room.

Henry shifts to stand, but I wave him off. "Let him have his space."

Instead of curling back into Kai, Henry leans forward and places his arms on his knees. "She needs him, Trev."

"And he needs her," I add, knowing we're all feeling the pressure to be on the same page.

"What about you?"

Kai's question has only one possible answer. Looking my friend in the eye, I give him my truth. "She's our heart. Of course I need her. I refuse to be far from her."

They nod, thoughtful once again. I just really fucking hope Ridge can sort his feelings and realize with Nina, with *us,* is where he's meant to be.

Chapter 24

Nina

I twist the deadbolt and turn the lock on the door handle. Their dull thuds match the sluggish beats of my aching heart.

The sound of my parents' car starting and eventually backing down my driveway slowly lowers the shutters on my feelings. This would be a time to process my feelings, as my therapist would say, but I can't. I refuse. These emotions are damaging and downright traumatizing.

It's like I've lost them all over again.

I'm alone in a house that suddenly feels freezing and empty. A chill works up my spine as silence slithers into my ears and chokes me until I'm mute. By the time I no longer hear their engine, I'm numb. Nothing but a shell that can't even feel the tears running down my cheeks.

I may as well be a robot for how stiff my legs are as they carry me to the living room. The sun shining through the window doesn't match the black hole that I have become, so like a thoughtless zombie, I close the shades.

As if that one task took the final shreds of my energy, my

knees buckle. The plush rug beneath me does nothing to soften the blow to my bones, but deep down I register that the fluffiness feels nice against my wet cheek as I curl up on my side.

They're gone. Today was their final day in town to make sure I settled in. And now Mom and Dad are just...*gone.* They're going home. *I want to go home.*

The wind must gust because the windows whistle in reminder that *this* is my home. Somewhere in the shade of my heavy weight of numbness, a flicker of sadness and discontent try to pull a sob from my throat, but all they do is make my tears fall faster.

I'm cold. *I want my mom.*

The wall creaks. *I want my dad.*

Alone...alone...alone...

Chapter 25

Ridge

The closer we get to Nina's house, the more my gut twists. "When did they leave?"

I've felt sick since the moment Meg called Henry. When Henry relayed Meg and Will's concerns for Nina since they left to go home today, we all abandoned our breakfast to head over there.

We've been showing up at her house for the past four days around lunchtime and haven't heard much from her parents since two days ago when we sat around the fire together.

"About an hour ago," Henry answers my question. I can't tell if his voice is tight or if it's just my energy twisting shit.

Fuck. Meg and Will's worries about how Nina would handle their departure seem to be rubbing off on me. I don't know this version of Nina. I have no idea what to expect if she *is* handling it poorly.

My idiot friends tell me I challenge Nina, but what the hell does that mean? All I hear is that I'm annoying and get on her nerves. Although, that isn't very different from when we were kids. Now that I think about it, she was always more cuddly with Henry, would never stop talking with Kai, and followed Trevor blindly.

When I put it that way, it feels like nothing has changed. *But it has.* I don't care that her spunk yesterday reminded me of fifteen-year-old Neen. That's not her anymore. The glare she gave me from the fucking corner of her couch had the power to incinerate me on the spot. Thankfully, I'm Nina proof. I thrive under her. *Fuck, not like that. Maybe like that.*

I did learn that while she doesn't like silence, she sure as shit doesn't like the volume of my video game turned up too loud. And *yes,* I did find her PS4 since it looks like we aren't going home anytime soon.

The thought of going home hurts me. I haven't said anything to the guys about moving here with them, even though I plan on doing exactly that. Trev's worried about me, but his energy needs to be on Nina. Just as mine does. And now it is.

Something about hearing my friends' devotion to the girl we grew up with and never forgot about shifted my priorities. Those people I know that are counting on us at work have other managers they can talk to. We did all the groundwork, built our resorts up to run themselves with amazing staff. It's time we move on.

It's time *I* move on and let go of some of the guilt that keeps Nina at arm's length.

We were kids. I was a teenager with such a vivid vision of the sketch I was doing that I didn't see the danger of letting Neen leave on her own. Or at least checking she got into Kai's car safely.

I was a child with a crush. Now I'm a man with some serious feelings and a whole heap of self-doubt. One thing for sure is love. I've always loved Nina and now I can't wait to figure out what makes her who she is.

The first step is bringing my walls down. So far, it fucking sucks.

"How much longer?" My throat feels thick, and swallowing doesn't help clear it up. Rubbing my chest does jack shit. "Fuck, I think I'm anxious."

Kai snorts next to me in the back of the SUV. My glare doesn't perturb him. It never does. "He says *I think I'm anxious.* Dude, you were in therapy for three fuckin' years. What do you mean you *think* you're anxious?"

"Children," Trevor scolds in the driver's seat while Henry fucking chuckles.

My hand clenches in a fist against my pounding heart. "Excuse the fuck out of you, Kai. Obviously I know when my anxiety is flaring up, asshole. This feels different."

"A sense of foreboding," Henry confirms.

"Yes!" I agree, nodding and adjust my glasses. "So, I repeat," I pause to glare at Kai again before asking my question from before he taunted me, "how much longer?"

Trevor answers me without poking my buttons. "Two minutes. We aren't barging in there. We'll knock and make sure she knows it's us, okay?"

No promises.

"Okaaay?" Trev draws out. When I glance up in the rearview mirror, I notice him raising his eyebrows at me. Instead of arguing, I nod and unbuckle my seatbelt so I can jump out.

A minute later, I'm hopping out of the vehicle before Trevor shifts into park. Kai is hot on my heals as I jog up to the front door.

"Her curtains are closed," Kai notices, and I know what he's saying.

Every time we've been here, they've been wide open. Nina's

need to keep an eye on her surroundings has been made obvious by the way she excessively monitors the neighborhood when she's on edge. Which is, unfortunately, more often than not.

"Nina! It's us! Let me in!" I shout like we've done every time, so she's somewhat at ease about opening the door.

After a about ten seconds of knocking and shouting with no response, I try the door handle. "Locked," I grumble.

"I'd be pissed if it wasn't," Trevor says sounding both proud and frustrated at the same time.

My skin feels like it's crawling. "I'm going around back."

"Me too," Henry adds and chases after me as I round her house. "Want a hand?" he offers when we come to a stop at her locked fence gate.

I don't reply as I put my foot into his waiting palms. Henry grunts as he lifts, and I jump. Cursing as I'm fucking *launched* into the air, I grapple to grab hold of a picket, but all I manage is an ungraceful landing in the grass on the other side of her eight-foot fence.

"What the hell, Hen?! Have you been working out?" I accuse, scrambling to my feet and fixing my lenses.

"Don't blame me, Ridge! I didn't know you could jump that fucking high!" Henry retorts.

Huffing and rubbing my hip, I unlatch the fence to let him inside. He doesn't spare me a glance as he sprints to the patio. It feels like I watch in slow motion as Henry bottles up all his energy and strength to wrench open the sliding glass door, only for it to be unlocked.

"Fuck!" he shouts, startled as he all but throws himself to the ground. Like he didn't just scrape the shit out of his knee *again*, he jumps up.

"The chaos," I mutter, half laughing, and beat him through the doorway.

"Trev's gonna be mad about the door," Henry whispers, following me.

"Kai's gonna be mad you ripped open your scab."

All humor dies as we round the kitchen island and don't see our girl. Until we rush into the living room.

And there she is.

"NINA!"

Chapter 26

Kai

I don't know how long Trevor and I wait, but it feels like an eternity passes before Ridge rips the front door open. One look at his pale complexion and I know something's really wrong.

Before I can ask, Trev rushes through the door and into the living room. Following him as fast as I can is out of the question and before I can fully grasp the situation in front of me, I'm gasping and panicking.

"Kai, turn the TV on and open the shades. Kai!"

Snapping out of my shock, I do as Trevor asks, but the tasks only distract me for a few moments. Now I'm back to feeling helpless as I watch my fiancé cradle Nina to his chest and rock her back and forth on the floor.

She's trembling so hard I think her teeth are going to ache if we can't get her to snap out of whatever trance she's in. Counting her tears is almost as painful as counting her blinks. Nina's cheeks are soaked and she hasn't stopped staring at a blank spot on the wall.

"Shh, Nina," Henry whispers when her jaw clacks a little

harder on her exhale. "You're okay. We're here now. You aren't alone."

"What do we do?" I can't stop staring and I swear I'm starting to shake just like she is. My nerves are going fucking haywire trying to *do* something, but I have no clue what I can do.

"Ridge," Trevor snaps, making Nina flinch. "Fuck, I'm so sorry, baby. Ridge, go get her a glass of water with a straw."

Like a useless piece of shit, I watch Trev hoist Henry up from behind and guide him to sit on the couch with Nina in his lap. The whimper she lets loose when Trevor's towering form enters her line of vision hurts my heart for him. *God, he looks like she just stabbed him in the soul.*

"It's only Trevor, pretty girl," Henry coos, petting her head while tucking her under his chin.

Ridge scurries into the living room with a big ass purple bottle mumbling, "Here," as he shoves it into Trevor's hands.

Bossy pants doesn't even look at me when he demands my next move. "Kai, turn the volume up and put that vampire show on that she likes. Henry, shift so she's looking at the TV. Maybe the bad guy with a British accent can coax her back."

I don't hesitate to follow Trev's guidance. He may be a bit overbearing, but he knows his shit and right now we really need some fucking help.

Nina still hasn't stopped crying, nor will she suck on the straw against her lips. Still unsure how to help, I stand and continue watching like a fucking idiot. At least Ridge had the thought of sitting on the floor in front of Henry.

My heart thunders and I can't help but wonder what the hell is going on inside her head. Still she cries, even ten minutes into the episode, no matter how many fangs are flashed.

A fuzzy haze seems to descend over my tired eyes and my ears have begun to block out Henry's gentle words and Trev's encouragement for her to drink some water. What snaps me out of my frozen stance is the same thing that makes Trev stiffen. Ridge reaches out and, oh so lightly, wraps his hand around Nina's bare foot that's dangling near his shoulder.

Nina sucks in a choked breath, and finally, *fucking finally*, focuses on something. Then...she moves.

I take a step forward when she tries to tug her foot free of Ridge's grasp, but he holds firm. We all watch with bated breath as he begins trailing his thumb along the sole of her foot. He's rubbing her scars and I swear to fuck my heart stops beating for fear that she's going to freak out.

The guys and I haven't talked about her poor destroyed feet or the scar on the back of her calf, but I think it's safe to say we're all still processing the amount of hurt our girl has survived. We haven't seen it all. I know that, and I'm aware the more skin she reveals, the more my heart is going to break. *Whippings,* Will had said.

To my absolute astonishment, Nina releases a shaky breath and relaxes into Ridge's hold. Ridge, like the risky fucker he is, kisses the top of her foot and continues watching the show.

Feeling dumb, I chew on my lip before finally taking a seat beside Henry and Nina.

"Drink." Trevor's voice is gruff. Nina looks him in the eye while she obeys, making him gulp. *Yeah...damn.*

Now's not the time to be getting any ideas, but watching her relax into us and our old dynamics makes my blood heat. *Fuck, I missed her.*

Sipping on her straw, she glances over her shoulder at Henry like it's the first time she noticed him. Henry smiles at her and tucks a wayward piece of her brown hair behind her ear. "Hi, pretty girl." When her eyes droop in response, he chuckles. "Rest, Neen. We'll watch over you."

My throat is thick with emotion, and it takes so much effort not to reach for her. Instead, I place my hand on my fiancé's knee and try to settle the anxiety that's been wreaking havoc on my system for too long to be healthy.

After a few minutes of watching Nina, Trev replaces his ass on the coffee table with the bottle. "She needs to eat something when she wakes up."

With a final glance at her, he nods like he needs to convince himself Nina will be safe while he's in the kitchen. Trev knows, just as we all do, that she will never be alone again.

We're here, surrounding her with motivation to live and love. She'll be okay. No. *Nina will be happy. We will make it so.*

Chapter 27

Nina

Now that I've been forced to nap, eat, and hydrate, I'm beginning to realize my behavior earlier was an over-reaction. But, gosh. Ignoring the demons that try to convince me I'm back there in hell is next to impossible. Especially when I have everything working against me.

Since Mom, Dad, and I spent the morning outside, the TV wasn't keeping the silence at bay when they left. I hadn't had a good night's sleep in a while, so my emotions were right there for the taking. And take the demons did. Watching my mom and dad walk out the door before hearing their car drive away from me was a new kind of torture.

At least when I was taken, I was leaving them against my will. This time, maybe for the first time ever, they chose to leave me and I...I let them. Because begging for them to stay or chasing after them isn't something an adult should do.

They believe in me, but that doesn't matter when I don't believe in myself. I don't *want* to live on my own. Breaking the barrier that prevents me from facing confrontation is one of the hardest things I've been trying to reverse.

I was whipped, hit, slapped, punched, and kicked whenever I opened my mouth while I lived with Mr. M because I had nothing to say beyond begging for my mom and dad. Pleading with the monster to let me go free ended in my first whipping. Swearing for the first and only time in my life resulted in a split lip and no food for four days. But alas, I needed to eat to have enough strength for my chores.

My chores. I wasn't joking when I told my mom that it's a good thing I know how to clean and cook. I did everything for that monster and got nothing in return. My skills are vast in a home, but, as my therapist would say, they weren't born of healthy intention.

Also, like she used to tell me, *it's not about knowing how to survive, but* wanting *to survive.* For a while there after my parents drove away, I don't think I wanted to survive.

Life without them down the hall or laughing at the dinner table is dull and scary. So when the locks clicked closed, and I was left in deafening silence, I cracked. Some days I believe I've shattered as much as I possibly can, other days like to prove me wrong. That was today.

Then something else happened; I handed some of those broken pieces to Ridge. Giving a few sharp ones to Henry was as easy as breathing air when he smiled down at me. Trevor stole a handful when he took charge, and Kai helped carry the scattered weight just by being near me.

"Nina?"

If I had a nickel for how many times someone says my dang name as a question...

"You okay?"

I would probably shrug if it wasn't Kai asking. I *do* shrug but I add, "Define okay."

Ridge is playing his video game while sitting on the floor in front of me again. I really want to run my hands through his hair, but I don't think—

Kai interrupts my thoughts as he collapses onto the couch a few inches away from me. "Like you could smile at me. That's how I would define it."

"Oh..." I murmur. *Why did that hurt so much? When was the last time I smiled?* "Sorry."

"No apologizing!" Trevor scolds from the kitchen, making me jump and grip my blanket harder.

I sigh. *Trevor has so many rules, almost like—No!* Trev is nothing like Mr. M. The rules he's trying to make me follow seem to only be for my benefit. There was *no* benefit to anything when I lived in that basement.

Different. This is different. Hopefully, if I keep reminding myself of that, my anxiety will lessen around them.

"Shit sticks on a fucking shroom bitch! UGH! NOOO NOT MY CAR!"

With each word Ridge bellows at his game, my eyes widen until a shocked laugh bursts out of my chest scaring me even more than Trevor's stern tone. Whipping around like *I'm* the car crash he can't help but watch, Ridge looks at me like he's never seen me before. That hurts too. *My gosh, that hurts so much.*

"Nina girl," he breathes with a growing grin. "I missed that sound."

Nibbling on my lip, I glance at Kai who gives me the courage to respond. "M-me too." I'm not talking about my laugh. I mean the big grin he always used to flash at me when he got his way.

Before I know what's happening, Ridge kisses my knee and spins around to restart his racing game. He used to love the zombie one, but he mumbled something about it being too gory to play here, and that's the last I heard of it.

"Mmm, that feels nice."

It's Ridge's moan that makes me realize my fingers are running through his hair. My belly sinks and I go to yank my hand away from his blond locks, but a firm grip stops me.

"He likes it," Henry whispers in my ear, having come from out of nowhere. I shiver and a blush heats my cheeks. He guides my hand to the top of Ridge's head again. "And you want to touch. So do it, pretty girl."

Once Henry has me petting his friend again, he releases me and takes a seat by Kai. They share a kiss and soft words. My eyes start to burn and I don't think I could get a word out if I tried. Instead of paying attention to Henry and his *fiancé*, I focus on making Ridge feel good. *Someone should.*

At least nobody's pushing me to answer questions I really don't want to answer. I'll take the win even if it hurts.

Chapter 28

Henry

"It's been a week. We need answers." Trevor looks so damn determined it makes me want to avoid challenging him. Especially while he's driving.

While I agree with his desire to know what happened the day we found Nina shaking on her living room floor, I don't think forcing her to tell us is appropriate. At least not a week later.

Since then, we've gone over there every day in between looking for a house to rent. It's been nice. Nina's slowly but surely coming out of her shell. I hate to say it, but I think her panic attack last week brought us closer.

It doesn't sound like much, but she's starting to touch the other guys a little. I've heard that beautiful giggle a few times, and we even got a snort yesterday when Ridge fucked up boiling noodles.

"What kind of answers, Trev?" Kai asks from beside me in the back of the SUV. "I don't think she's gonna want to talk about last week."

"Isn't it obvious what happened?" Ridge honestly seems

confused. Glancing between the three of us from the passenger seat up front, he frowns. "Will and Meg had *just* left; officially leaving her for the first time ever. The TV wasn't on, which left her in silence. And she was on the ground."

Trevor narrows his gaze on the road as he thinks through the meaning behind his cousin's words. "But why was she on the ground? Why were the drapes closed?"

"She was back there..." I whisper, the realization truly dawning on me for the first damn time. "Oh god. She was alone, her parents getting further and further away. The house was silent, and the sun didn't fit the scenario she was stuck in."

Kai grabs and squeezes my hand. "Nina was back in the basement."

Ridge nods in the front seat. "She was triggered, Trevor."

"Well, then we need to know what her triggers are!" Trev snaps, white knuckling the steering wheel.

Scowling, Ridge throws his hands in the air. "There's a high probability that asking her could be a trigger. *And* she might not even *know* what they are! Let her open up in her own time."

"I agree," I add, trying my best to meet Trevor's intense gaze in the rearview mirror. Luckily we're almost at Nina's house so I can make a quick escape. "Let her open up in her own time."

Grumbling and scratching at his neat beard, Trevor gets us into Nina's driveway safely. Excited to see my girl, I'm out and closing the door immediately. Then the strangest fucking thing happens. The garage door opens, which it never does.

I knew Nina had her own car because Ridge went snooping one of the first days we came to see her, but we've only seen her in her living room, in the kitchen or out on the patio.

My heart thunders in my ears as Nina reverses her cute white Jeep Compass. Ever so slowly, she inches her way down the driveway, being exceptionally careful of the four of us now standing in her driveway.

When Nina comes to a stop beside us, she rolls down the driver's side window. Her light brown waves are messy, like when we were kids, and the freckles on her nose and cheeks stand out beautifully in the natural light.

"Hi," she says, offering us a shaky smile. Unfortunately, that's common. I hate how unsure my pretty girl is.

We each say our hellos, but Trev asks, "Where are you off to, baby?" I can practically see the vein in his neck pumping. We've all gotten used to Nina being at home where we know she's safe and comfortable. This is new territory for us. *Why is she leaving now?*

Nina's face falls, and she glances around nervously. "Oh. I-I'm sorry. I just...I have an appointment."

"What kind of appointment?" Ridge cocks his head, his messy hair flopping over his eyebrow.

"Um..." Nina mumbles and nibbles on the inside of her cheek.

Idiots. "Neen, you don't need to answer that. We just want to make sure you're okay."

She nods immediately, but the tremble of her bottom lip has me and Trevor stepping forward. "Want company?" *Shit, maybe I'm being too pushy now.* Nina makes us protective and possessive.

"It's just my annual physical," Nina explains, looking embarrassed and wildly unsure. I bet Trevor wants to rip her out of the car to feed her pancakes and milk until she falls asleep. *Christ,* I'm bordering on that reaction.

"Good girl," Trevor rumbles, reaching into the car and rubbing his thumb along her cheekbone. She shivers and my cock stirs in my pants. "Now answer Henry's question."

"I'm sorry. What—" Her breath catches when Trev pets her plump bottom lip.

I can't stop my smirk. Making a mental note to get my fiancé to rail me later, I answer her unspoken question. "Want company?"

"She does," Trevor decides for her when she thinks for a moment too long.

I raise a brow and she whispers, "Yes please".

Trevor releases her from the sexual tension that I didn't even realize we could fucking create by stepping back and cooing sweet praises at her. I hear her huff out a big breath of air just as I open the passenger side door and settle myself in the seat beside her.

"Alright. No speeding, baby girl," Trevor demands.

Kai blows us a kiss and Ridge wishes her luck at the doctor. As soon as her window closes, the tension in the car steadily grows. Soft music plays through her speakers as she diligently drives us the ten minutes to her clinic without saying a word.

I hate how nervous she looks. The light tinge of pink on her cheeks makes me wonder if there was another reason for the tension in the car. The small space between us as we head into the building feels like a live wire.

I don't give myself a chance to second guess what I do next. I grab her hand in mine, guide her to the front desk, and say her name to the young man at the computer.

Almost like she's in a daze, Nina follows me and answers my questions as I fill out the forms, since this is her first time seeing a new doctor. My heart races the entire time. I'm so on edge that I think I'm shaking. This feels like a monumental moment in our relationship and for Nina to be branching out into the world.

So when she goes back with the nurse, albeit reluctant to let my hand go, I make a promise to myself and Nina that I won't let her hole up at home any longer. It's time she lives again.

Chapter 29

Nina

I t's hard to believe anyone enjoys going to the doctor. Add severe anxiety on top of a depressing lack of social skills, and going to the doctor feels absolutely terrifying. And awkward. So, so awkward.

Thankfully, Henry doesn't ask questions as I approach him in the lobby. When he steals the keys from my hand, *I* want to ask questions, but I've hit my limit.

Unfortunately, my reprieve doesn't last long enough for me to buckle my seatbelt. "Nina, are you okay? You look really flushed. Are you sick?"

I bet my toes turn beet red, too. *My gosh, what do I say?* "No, I'm not sick." There, I answered his question. Maybe now he'll take me home.

Yet he still doesn't put the car in drive. "Okay, then..."

"Henry, I'm fine, okay?" Dread descends, making my heart hammer in my chest and my eyes widen. "I'm sorry!" I quickly add as fear strips me of all thought process beyond the fact that I snapped at him.

Oh my gosh, I snapped at a man. I don't do confrontation.

Why didn't I just tell him?! I'll tell him! Anything to get the frown wiped from his beautiful face.

"I had to get my IUD taken out because it's been in for too long and now they don't want to replace it since there's a high probability it's messing with my weight and definitely my hormones which might be influencing my appetite and anxiety and—"

"Woah, pretty girl. Take a deep breath," Henry coos, grabbing my hand and pressing my palm to his chest. "There you go. In and out....What is it that Trev likes to say? Ah, yes. *Good girl.*"

My calming breaths shift into an airy giggle as my tummy flutters. Trevor does like to say that to me, especially when I take a bite from his hand. *Is that weird?*

"No, it's not weird." *I guess I voiced my thoughts.* Henry smiles and rubs his thumb along the back of my hand. "Trev has some Daddy Dom tendencies."

My eyes widen in shock, but Henry just laughs and continues. "No, he doesn't like to be called *Daddy*, but I bet he wouldn't mind if you called him Sir." He winks. "And are you really surprised? Even as a fifteen-year-old he was feeding you, making sure you were warm, and had the general traits of someone who likes to take care of others. As he's gotten older, those things have become a pillar of who he is. I can't speak for in the bedroom, but maybe just be prepared for Trev to take the lead."

My eyebrows are still in my hairline. "W-what? Why are you telling me this?"

Honestly, I'm not sure what's happening. I just spilled the beans about my embarrassing doctor's visit and now we're talking about Trevor's sexual preferences. I'm not naïve, even if I am a virgin. Thankfully, my sexual side is fully functioning since that's the only part of me that wasn't abused or taken advantage of.

Have I thought about the guys in *that* way? Yes. Since I was a teen and haven't stopped. Sometimes fantasizing about them late at night while I...touch myself is the only way I can get a few hours of sleep.

Would I take that step? Yes, BUT, does my anxiety cripple my confidence? Double yes. And could I choose? No. *But Henry and Kai did.*

Blinking away the upsetting inner monologue before I ruin my already unhinged mood, I focus back on Henry's probing gaze. "Neen, come on. You know we all had a crush on you." *Do I know that?* "Time hasn't changed our feelings."

OUR?!

"I'm sorry for pushing about the appointment," Henry continues like he didn't just drop a confusing bomb on me. "I'm worried about what they said about your weight and hormones. The fact that they didn't replace the IUD is also worrisome. I hope they talked through the side effects and you asked questions."

I nod, just like I did through most of my appointment. It's easier to agree than to explain that I didn't even know what to ask. *I want my mom.* I make a mental note to call her as Henry starts the car with a lingering glance at me.

"I'm here if you want to talk about anything or if you just need a snuggle, okay?"

"Okay," I whisper, and scold my aching uterus for perking up at the thought of being close to him.

As we're exiting the parking lot, Henry grins at me. "Let's meet the guys for lunch. What do you say?"

No. I don't say that, though. Instead, I twist my hands in my lap and nibble on my lip. I can give him some of the truth and maybe he can decide. "I don't feel very good, Hen," I murmur. "Taking it out, it, um, it hurt."

Concern furrows his brow, and he steals my left hand back. "I didn't think of that. Thank you for telling me, Nina. I'm proud of you for opening up."

What?

"I'll tell Trev to get some ice cream. Be ready for alpha male spoon feeding while we snuggle."

Two of them are getting married and the other two don't want you, my insecurities roar.

My anxiety takes a back seat when Henry kisses my hand and places it on his thigh. My body flushes with some form of neediness I don't think I've ever actually experienced.

I don't recognize myself without the trembles and self-deprecating thoughts. But I think I might like this new form of intimacy. Can I handle more?

Chapter 30

Trevor

Fucking hell. You know, I've been horny before, obviously, but I can barely control myself right now.

Kai chuckles but shuts up when I shoot him a vicious glare. He has a fucking fiancé to take care of his raging hard on when we go back to the hotel, but I don't. Neither does Ridge and he's barely concealing his hard on.

"Mmm," Nina moans around the spoon I plop between her lips. Her eyes are closed and her chest rises with her pleased inhale after swallowing down the cream. The tip of her pink tongue pokes out, and she sighs, wiggling back against Henry even more.

A clank draws my attention to my cousin again. "We're done with ice cream! Now. Everyone. Hand it over."

Kai laughs again, but I'm conflicted. I'd like to keep feeding Nina her treat, but a very large part of me wants to feed her something else.

"Yep." I clear my throat and hand Ridge Nina's spoon. "All done over here." I cough again and adjust myself as discreetly as possible.

Ridge grunts, takes away all the ice cream, and all but rushes from the living room.

"Uh, rude," Henry grumbles from his spot behind Nina. I wasn't jealous of him before for getting snuggles since I wanted to feed our girl, but I just gave that up because my libido couldn't hang.

"I agree..." Nina pouts, but I swear there's a little mischief in her eye.

I shift, pull one knee up on the cushion, and drape my arm around the back of the couch until I'm facing her. "Baby girl," I growl. "Were you teasing us with those little noises?"

Her eyes widen and her mouth pops open. I'm starting to worry I may have read into this all wrong, then Henry chuckles burying his face in her neck.

"Henry he-he—"

Henry kisses her cheek from behind. "I encouraged her to hum a few times. I bet her you guys wouldn't last five minutes without taking it away."

"Babe!" Kai's bark of laughter makes Nina blush.

Turning my heated stare on the dainty girl in front of me, I *encourage* her to open up to me. "And what was your bet, Nina?" Her lips twist, and she closes her eyes. I tug her hands away from her face when she tries to cover her rosy cheeks. "No, no. You wanted to play games. Tell me how long you thought we could hold out before we couldn't take your breathy little moans anymore."

Part of me is terrified that we're pushing too far. Henry sent a message earlier saying she had a rough appointment but not to worry. Obviously, I'm still worried.

He also told us she needed a distraction since she wasn't feeling well and he may have started pushing the boundaries we've put in place with her. We weren't going to pursue anything beyond building our friendship again, but leave it to

Henry to broach the topic of my dominant lifestyle. I was shocked and a little mad until he followed his text up with an explanation that Nina seemed a little turned on when he talked about it with her.

Kai hasn't stopped fucking teasing me about it since. Not to mention the tension in my body is only ratcheting up higher the longer my cock throbs in my damn shorts. Thank fuck Ridge took away the damn spoon and cream. I probably would have lost myself had we kept going.

Also, what the fuck is up with Henry pushing our buttons today? And what gave him the green light to start pushing Nina's?!

"Nina didn't think you would notice or care if she made an enticing show of licking your spoon, Trev." Henry gives me a cheeky grin and my jaw clenches at the meaning behind his words.

To Kai, I say, "You better spank his ass tonight."

Between bouts of laughter, he says, "We don't do that shit. But maybe if he begs for it, I'll warm his cheeks."

"Um," Nina squeaks and tries to get up off the couch. She doesn't get very far with the family snuggler wrapped around her like a koala.

Henry shushes her and pushes me back with his fucking knee. "Shh, the sexy vampire is about to carry her out of the hospital."

Just like that, the tension dissipates and the two trouble-makers dive back into the fictional world where the bad boys get the girls.

Kai watches Henry and Nina with warmth and love in his eyes. My heart squeezes at the realization that some things haven't changed. Maybe Henry saw a bit of the old Nina earlier and took that as his green light to take things up a notch.

I just hope Nina's ready because the four of us aren't going to be able to hold back for long. Not after her sexy display with her frozen snack.

Chapter 31

Nina

Ridge: Hi

I can't stop the gasp from spilling from my mouth. *Why is he texting me in the middle of the night?*

We just swapped numbers last week. Apparently, over three weeks of not having a way to contact me when they aren't here was no longer allowed. Trevor's words.

Honestly, the only people I text or call are my parents, so I didn't think to have another form of communication with the guys. And social media is off the table and forever will be for me.

I get the security information I need from the detectives and officers on Mr. M's case when they think he's on the move. I really don't need to read the articles about him making his way across the Canadian border. The girls aren't lasting anywhere near as long as I did. What he does to those girls after they've served their purpose? The same purpose I was used for...*I refuse to think about it.*

I already know every single detail because he used to

taunt me with what would happen once I got too weak to do my chores. The brutal treatment up to the point where my usefulness ended would seem like a day on the beach, he used to say.

I hate that I lasted so long.

Is it my fault he's killing faster? Did I anger him when I escaped and these girls are taking punishments meant for me?

I remember wishing that when the time came, I could have one final ray of sunshine to warm my face.

So it's in the darkness that I fear I'll never feel the sun again. Gulping and without any thought to what I'm doing, I type a response.

> Hi.

His response is immediate, and it makes me sink further into my bed.

> Ridge: I didn't think you'd be awake. Why aren't you asleep, Nina girl?

I don't hesitate, too caught up in the feel of having someone to talk to while I spiral. Mom thinks I should ask for help when I need it, and Dad wholeheartedly believes I can trust the guys.

> I'm scared...

> Ridge: Scared of what, Nina? What's going on?

Before I can tap my thumb once, Ridge's caller ID pops up on my screen. *Shoot, he's calling me? Texting is so much easier.* Reminding myself that at least he's not here to see my cry in person, I accept the call.

"Nina? Are you okay?"

He sounds so panicked it makes me feel bad. "I'm sorry, Ridge," I whisper. "Everything's fine. Sorry for worrying you."

"Stop apologizing and tell me what's wrong," he demands, voice hard and unrelenting.

Studying the shadows of my room that the hallway light creates, I feel my belly twist with anxiety. "Nights are hard, that's all."

Maybe if I downplay what keeps me up every night, he won't think I'm a freak. Or high maintenance. My lip wobbles. Learning that I'm not a burden was tough and, honestly, there are days I forget all the work I've done to let go of my negative thoughts.

Ridge doesn't pause and, if anything, the sounds from his end of the line become a bit muffled. "Why are the nights hard?"

"Why do you ask so many questions?" My heart beats rapidly, but it's slowly shifting from fear of the tall dark spot by my closet to exhilaration of bantering with my friend.

"Answer the question, Nina."

My vagina flutters in response to his unwavering tone. *Friends!* Since my attention is split between keeping an eye on the darkness and scolding my now wet panties, my filter slips. "Sometimes I worry I'll never see the sun again. That I'll never hear the birds chirping and get annoyed when the wind messes up my hair."

"Neen..." he breathes, but he's a distant sound now, as is the thud that accompanies his emotion.

"When it's dark out and I'm *supposed* to be asleep...in my room...I'm reminded of the basement. I had to be down there unless it was to clean or cook something for Mr. M. I—" My breath stutters out of me and the truth follows. "I never knew what time of day it was. There was only one lightbulb and no way of knowing until I was dragged up the steps. Then when I was thrown back down, I feared I would never know what the outside felt like."

"Nina—"

Sobbing with my heart verbally opening itself and begging to be put back together, I tell Ridge my deepest, darkest sin. "Many times I didn't want to know either. I just wanted it to end. I wanted all the pain to end, Ridge."

"Nina. Open the front door, right fucking now!"

I startle and fly into a sitting position when a few loud bangs sound from downstairs. "I-is that you at th-the door?"

"Yes. Let me in. You have one minute before I break it down, Nina girl. I'm coming in whether you invite me or not."

I'm scrambling out of bed before I think it through, but my mind still races as my feet carry me down the stairs. "Why a-are you here?" My hiccup breaks apart my words.

He doesn't respond, and the line goes dead just as I unlock all the safety features. I barely touch the handle before the door is being nudged open and a frantic Ridge is stepping into my house before locking the door behind him.

Turning back around, he looks ready to explode, but I don't take a step back. My throat closes over instead, and I so badly want to leap into his arms. He studies me for a beat as my tears continue to slide down my cheeks and onto my white T-shirt.

"Up."

"Wha—" I don't have a moment to be confused by his caveman speak because in the next nanosecond, his hands are under my butt and he's lifting me toward his body. My legs wrap around him naturally while my arms scramble to grab hold of his neck. "Oh my gosh," I huff and hold on as tight as I can while he stomps up the steps.

He doesn't say a freaking word, just tucks an arm under my butt and grabs hold of the banister as he climbs. I have never felt so small or...treasured. Watching his hard features and watery eyes, I melt into his protective embrace.

What happens next is completely out of my control and since we're at the top, safe and sound, I don't worry too much about the risk of it. My nose nudges the rim of his glasses back up his nose.

If I was blushing before my body turns to flame when his soulful golden eyes meet mine. "Do that again." His voice is so husky as he stops just inside of my dimly lit bedroom. I frown, but he wiggles his nose until his glasses shift down again. "Again, Nina."

I thought Trev was the bossy one. Still, I do as he asks. The cool metal of the rims makes the tip of my nose tingle, but Ridge's heavy, hot exhale blowing against my lips steals the chill.

I'm a raging inferno.

Chapter 32

Ridge

My phone hasn't stopped buzzing since I ran out of the hotel suite, but I couldn't care less about the others right now. All that matters is the woman in my arms looking at me like I could be the answer to all her problems. Fuck do I wish to be.

"Ridge," Nina whispers, her blue-grey eyes mere inches from mine. The way she's waiting for me to do something has my cock twitching in my pants, but thankfully she's seated just above so she can't feel what she does to me.

Too soon. I fucking hate that reminder, but it's true. Not to mention I sped my way over here because Nina's scared. *Not* because she asked me to eat her hot cunt.

"Mmm. Okay, Nina girl." I pat her ass with my hand and plop her on the bed in the far side of her room. "Stay here for a second while I go grab a few things."

Like the little minx Nina's proving to be, she scurries to her knees and crawls toward me as I start walking away. "You'll come back?"

My fucking heart. Nina's confused frown and tilted head are so adorable I'm unable to resist going back to her. "Always," I confirm and press a kiss to the corner of her mouth.

I turn on my heel when she sucks in a surprised breath because if I don't walk away now I'm liable to tackle her and figure out what other noises she will make for me.

My phone buzzes in rapid succession, propelling me down the stairs. I don't have to check the messages to know all three of them are outside of Nina's house right now. I barely have the door unlocked before Trevor is barreling into me like a fucking caveman and demanding answers.

Shoving him back a step, I glance up the stairs to make sure Nina isn't watching. "Be quiet, man. For fuck's sake."

I watch Kai lock the door once again. Honestly, I have no idea what I expected when I caused a ruckus getting out of the hotel, but having them here pulls me back from the feral edge a little.

"Is she alright?" Henry asks, looking like he's about to go check on Nina himself.

Sighing, I rub the back of my neck. "She's scared of the dark. Of nighttime, really. Then she was telling me about...about her time in that basement. There's some really fucked up shit to unpack there. The only solution I could think of was to watch over her so she could sleep."

The three of them stare at me for a moment before they kick off their shoes. I'm not about to tell them everything she unloaded tonight, not when my girl is upstairs waiting for me.

Trev's gaze is probing when he stands back up from untying his tennis shoes. "Did something happen between the two of you?"

I meet his stare head on and ignore the smirk on Kai's face. "I held her, she didn't panic. She actually pushed my glasses back up my face with her nose. There was definite tension. Oh, and I kissed her."

"You what?! Ridge, she's not ready for that!" Trevor hisses, advancing on me.

I stand my ground. In no way does he have a say in how I pursue Nina. "Calm down Trevor. Nina doesn't need this kind of energy right now. And I kissed the corner of her lips. But honestly, Trev, I read her cues accurately and knew not to push further than I did. If this is going to work with all of us, we need to trust one another."

"Ridge?"

Fuck. Turning around, I see Nina halfway down the stairs clutching a blanket to her chest. "Nina, I told you to stay."

To my surprise, she glowers at me and retorts, "I'm not a dog."

"Definitely not a dog," I agree, unable to hold back my grin. Henry steals her attention with a wave and a soft hello.

"I want to know what you meant," Nina says, her voice wavering slightly after she greets Henry and Kai.

Why did she have to fucking hear that?

Thankfully, my cousin steps in before I spill my guts. "Tomorrow, baby. For now, Ridge is going to keep you company so you can sleep and the three of us will keep watch down here, okay?"

"But why?" She genuinely seems confused why we would stay. "I mean, like...why do you care if I sleep or not?"

Well, fuck. How many times can one person break my damn heart?

Trevor's face falls, then turns to stone. "Come here, Nina."

"So demanding," Kai mumbles, making Henry laugh under his breath.

Henry's response is so fucking accurate. "But she's so beautiful when she obeys him."

That's putting it mildly. With a blush on her cheeks and her fingers digging into her blanket, she pads down the stairs and stops about a foot away from us.

Kai beats Trev by stepping into Nina's space and tucking a stand of hair behind her ear. "We care about you because we love you, Nina."

Her brown eyebrows furrow again, making me want to slam my head into the wall. It feels like we're messing this up and completely failing at communicating. Clearly, our casual fucking answers only add to her confusion.

"We'll talk about it in the morning," I interrupt before she gives herself a headache overthinking Kai's statement. I grab her bicep and immediately feel like an ass when she flinches. "Shit, I'm sorry."

"It-it's okay," she appeases and takes a steadying breath. "Just maybe go slow when you grab me?" The urge to encourage her to truly *state* her needs is strong, but that's a goal for later.

I nod and apologize once again, but I don't linger on the moment. Turning her back toward the stairs, I place my hand on her lower back and nudge her to get moving. "You need to sleep. Come on."

She doesn't fight me as she climbs the stairs after saying thank you to the others. In a daze, she crawls back into her bed and snuggles down into her pillows looking absolutely exhausted. I wonder if this happens every night where she stays awake scared until her body finally gives out and forces her to sleep.

It's not the time to ask questions, though. Instead I check her closet, ensuite bathroom, and under her bed. "All clear, Neen," I report and settle onto the window bench seat to keep an eye on her.

All she does is nod and curl into the fetal position. I hold her gaze until her eyelids take over and force her under. "Good night," I whisper and swallow down the emotion that threatens my composure. "I missed you," I can't resist from adding just as I can't stop a tear from slipping free.

I *missed her so much.*

Chapter 33

Nina

"Where do you work?" Ridge jumps and I suppress a laugh. I've been awake for a bit just watching him as he types away on his phone. Feeling bad for startling him, I say, "Sorry."

"Christ. Why are you awake? You only slept for an hour and a half, Nina."

I won't tell him it was much less than that, so I only shrug.

Frowning at me with the light from the hallway lighting his way to my bedside, he strides to me and sits by my knees. "You should try to sleep more," he murmurs, slowly placing his hand on my thigh.

The weight feels nice on my leg, but I'm too wrapped up in everything that I don't know about the man who kissed me earlier. "Tell me about you, Ridgie. Please."

I'm the worst person ever. I've strategically avoided asking any questions about the four of them out of fear that I would find myself unworthy of their attention. Connecting with people is hard in general, plus I know what happens when I make meaningful connections only for them to die in a shallow grave of decaying hope.

Ridge watches me for a moment before gently reclining over my legs with his elbow propping him up behind my knees. "What do you want to know?"

My eyes burn with so much sadness for all the time we lost. "Everything. Please."

"Well, Trev and I own Neen Resorts." My eyes widen at the name and the sheer accomplishments they've made. "It was a lot of fucking work, I tell ya. But our recruitment team has been a lifesaver. We have some amazing managers and people capable of running everything when we're busy. Trev likes to go to meetings I say they're boring as fuck, but I like to go to the design ones."

"Ridge, that's amazing. The name..."

He gives me a gentle nod and smile. "You, Nina. We named it after you. When we were at BYU getting our business degrees, our main goal was to form a business with your name as the headline. You were never far from our thoughts."

"I—" My tears are unstoppable as it finally hits me just how much I've missed out on. "Gosh, I'm sorry." I groan and wipe my face as I wiggle out from under him.

"Please don't apologize, Nina girl. I want all of you, so don't hold back those feelings on my account, please."

Groaning, I rub the heels of my palms into my burning eyes. "You guys keep saying stuff like that and I don't get it."

The bed moves, and heat suddenly engulfs my wrists before my hands are tugged away from my face. "You really won't go back to sleep, huh?" Ridge asks seriously. I shake my head. *Not a chance.* "Then let's go see if the other three are awake and willing to make us omelets."

"**D**id all of you go to BYU?" Asking the question that burns a hole in my heart is hard, but I have to make myself ask the heartbreaking questions if we're going to move forward.

Brigham Young University was where the four of us promised we would go to college together. *I broke my promise...*

"No," Kai admits and takes a big gulp of his coffee. "I lived with Henry, Ridge, and Trevor, but I never went to college. I have a traveling blog that does really damn well."

Henry beams at Kai with far more energy than Kai could ever gather before six in the morning. "He's living his dream," Henry gushes.

That familiar ache in my chest whenever I see their love for one another is back. I feel so dang guilty that it hurts to have lost them to each other.

"Henry got an art degree and graduated a year before us," Trevor announces with pride in his voice. "He restores old books. And he creates amazing special edition covers for authors."

"Wow! Really?!" The excitement buzzing through my veins is like a drug. "Oh! I wonder if I've seen any of your work. What authors do you work with?!"

The silence doesn't deter me. Feeling invigorated for the first time since, who knows, I leap from the couch and bolt for the stairs. "I'm gonna grab my e-reader!"

With my e-reader in my hand, I run down the stairs only to be swept off my feet as soon as I reach the bottom. "Hey!" I squeal and I swear my heart yelps.

"Naughty Nina," Trevor growls in my ear. He releases me a moment after my panties dampen. "Don't ever run down the stairs like that again. You could have gotten seriously hurt."

Trevor standing in front of me with a scowl etched into his hard features makes me gulp. His straight and styled dirty blond hair and perfectly trimmed beard give him an aura of authority that I am helpless to ignore.

"I'm sorry," I say. "I was just so excited."

His blue eyes soften. "I know, baby. I don't want you to get hurt ever again, so I need you to be careful."

"Okay." Shoot, I feel bad for scaring him. I debate my next move for half a second before I grab his hand. "I'll be more careful."

His hand shifts and something cold brushes my skin. Curious, I look down and the world stops moving.

"T-Trevor...my ring," I gasp and yank his pinky up to my face. "You're wearing my ring."

"Yeah, Nina. I've worn it since your sixteenth birthday and haven't taken it off since," he confirms.

"I left it in your truck when we went to the beach the day before," I murmur, remembering the last time I wore my silver band.

Memories flash through my head of our beautiful day in the sun. I can still feel the way his big hands held my waist and the brush of Ridge's fingers along my thigh. Kai had kissed my shoulder, and Henry heated my bare skin with his heavy gaze. Their attention made me spacey, and for the first time in many, many years, I left my ring behind in Trevor's truck.

"I wore it on my thumb." Absentmindedly, I notice he wears it on his smallest finger; a clear representation of our size differences. "I can't believe you've kept it all this time."

Looking up, I startle and suck in a breath at the intense look in his eyes. "We've all kept you close, baby girl."

"A-all of you?" I stutter, just now noticing the other guys standing around me and Trevor.

"I have your first initial tatted on my right hip bone where you hit me with a baseball in high school." Ridge lifts his shirt and tugs his shorts down a little, showing off the dainty N inked into his skin.

My mouth goes dry and my soul feels like it opens wide to accept him into my life for good.

"I have a rock collection like you used to have," Henry admits next. "And Kai has air fresheners, candles, diffusers, and scent rollers that all smell like roses."

Roses...My scent of choice.

"I—" My voice catches as I look at each of the men opening their hearts to me. "I don't know what to say."

"Then you really aren't gonna know how to respond to this next part," Ridge teases and looks at Henry. *Was this planned? I just wanted to talk about books.*

"Nina, we love you. And before you brush that off, we're *in love* with you. All four of us. We are hoping you still feel the same way we do after getting to know us again this past month." Henry makes it sound so...normal.

"I don't—"

Ridge cuts me off and leans against the banister. "That dirty book you were reading a few weeks ago, I looked it up. Learned *a lot* about why choose romance. That's what this is. That's what we're talking about."

"That's fiction," I say, aghast and feeling like I'm in some warped wet dream. Because believe me, my heart and vagina definitely love the sound of this.

"Pretty sure it's called polyamory," he fires back.

I open my mouth to tell him he's crazy, but the alarm on my phone blares in the pouch of my sweatshirt. My ears cringe and

Ridge's frown turns into one of disgust as he steals my phone out of my hand and shuts the godawful noise off.

"Why in the hell is *that* your alarm? And why the fuck do you have an alarm at six am when you don't get enough sleep to begin with?"

My lips purse with annoyance. Snatching my phone back, I fold my arms. "Pretty sure it's called being an adult." *Gosh, he pushes my dang buttons!*

"We'll revisit this discussion," Trevor announces.

My glare travels from one man to the next. "My alarm isn't a problem."

Trev's lips twitch. "I wasn't talking about your horrendous choice of an alarm. I mean we will talk about our relationships later once we've all had some rest."

"Come," Henry says softly as he wraps an arm around my waist. "Snuggle with me while we figure out who turns into a vampire next."

We both know who it's going to be, but rewatching my favorite show with Henry is like watching it for the first time again. It makes me wonder how many firsts we can recreate.

Plus, it's the perfect distraction from the building tension between the four of us. But how long until it snaps?

Chapter 34

Kai

I t's been a week since we tried to express our intentions to Nina. Seven days of her brushing the conversation off like we don't actually mean what we're saying. It's infuriating. We're men, we know what we want and we want her. *But what if she doesn't want us?*

"You're thinking awfully hard," Henry rumbles sleepily in my ear. I bite back a moan when his fingers dip into the waistband of my boxers. "Lemme see what else is hard."

"Fuck," I curse, my hips bucking when his hot hand grabs hold my aching cock.

Humming, he licks the back of my neck. "So hard, Kai. Is this all for me, or is it for Nina? Or," he teases, pumping me expertly, "maybe you're thinking about me tongue fucking our girl's sweet cunt while you rail my ass from behind."

My body heats and my neck arches. "Henry," I groan his name and ungracefully shove my hand down his boxers. "Fuck. *Fuck!*"

He thrusts into my grip, his precum helping him glide effortlessly through my fingers.

"Mmmhmmm. What if she were here right now, watching us fuck each other's fists? I would have her kneeling in front of you while she bounces on her fingers. I bet her tits are a perfect handful. Bet her nipples would pebble on your tongue nicely."

Motherfucking son of a—When Henry gets into dirty talk, he *really* gets into it and it's impossible to keep my cool. He may be my sweet nerd, but he can top like a fucking rock star when the mood arises.

And the mood fucking rose.

"Would you want our sweet Nina to sit on your face, Kai?" His voice has dropped a few octaves as his pleasure begins to peak.

Pressure builds at the base of my spine and my balls draw up. "Shit. I'm gonna come." Tingles race from my head to my toes, making them curl as my whole body stiffens.

Henry thrusts into my hand, moaning while he too comes close to the edge. It's hot, it's dirty, it's absolutely—

"Come. NOW," he groans, his warm cum splashing against my lower back.

The tingles intensify as if waiting for Henry's command. My vision darkens and air catches in my throat. Coming so fucking hard I go silent, wave after wave of pleasure courses through my body.

"Mmm," Henry hums. "Good morning."

I turn to catch his lips with mine. Once I'm done peppering his mouth with kisses, I praise, "You are so damn sexy, you know that?"

He fucking blushes, making my soft cock twitch with interest. "Yeah, I woke up with a bit of energy, huh?"

A laugh bursts from my chest. "You, me, and the other two, we're all liable to go a little feral after being around our girl for so long."

Henry groans and buries his face in the pillow. "The sexual tension is killing me, Kai."

I flip around, trying to ignore the stickiness on my back and focus on soothing my fiancé instead. Still, I chuckle at his poutiness. Petting his head, I say, "I know, Hen. But imagine how wound up Trev and Ridge must be."

"Poor fuckers," he agrees, his words muffled in the pillow.

Laughing, I spank his ass and roll out of bed. "Come on, time to get up. Lots to do today!"

Henry's fake snore follows me into the bathroom. *God, I love him.*

Henry and I are standing outside of the second house we're looking at today with matching frowns.

"I don't like it," he says. "It's over twenty minutes away from Nina's house."

Crossing my arms, I try to think of any other option. "I know, but we *need* somewhere to live and I refuse to go home. Ugh," I groan before kicking a rock. "We need to put the other house on the market, but all of our shit is there."

"We could hire someone," Henry offers, still glaring at the nice house in front of us.

"Or we could go back for a week—"

Whipping toward me, Henry scowls. "No. We aren't leaving Nina."

"Alright," I soothe, wrapping him in my arms. "I was just thinking through our options. We have to get this sorted, though. We've been at the resort for far too long."

"I want to be as close to Neen as possible." The emotion in

Henry's voice makes my throat clog with my own worries. "We love her. We should be *with* her."

My heart constricts painfully. "Four men in love with the same woman. Two of whom are getting married. How do we convince her our family isn't complete without her between us?"

"Million dollar question," Henry whispers, snuggling into my chest.

The four of us have always known Nina is the love of our souls. That didn't change when Henry and I got together. While it hurt to acknowledge that we may never have Nina be a part of our love, we still made a point to talk about what we would have wanted if Nina was ever found.

Bottom line, Henry, Trevor, Ridge, and I are in love with Nina. The ramifications of sharing aren't as overwhelming as our need for our woman.

As if our thoughts conjured her, Nina's soft voice wraps around us with awe and a hint of caution. "You're in love with me?"

Henry and I jolt, then twist around in shock. Nina stands in front of Trevor and Ridge who both look shocked. With her arms wrapped around her waist in a tight white long sleeve shirt and flowy capri pants, she looks stunning even if I can tell she's too warm.

"Nina, what are you—"

"Ah," Ridge cuts in. "Meg called me and asked us to get Nina out of the house for some fresh air. So we thought we would meet up with you two. Maybe surprise you with our Nina girl."

"Well, this is quite a surprise," I joke, trying to lighten the mood even with Nina still staring me down.

She steps forward and tightens her arms around her waist. "Is what you said true, Kai?" I hate seeing how uncertain and small she looks right now. "Four men in love with me? You guys aren't complete without me? What does that even mean?"

Henry shifts slightly. "Maybe we should head back—"

"No." Nina releases her waist and lifts her chin. "Tell me now."

"I just think—"

She cuts Henry off again. "*I* just think you turned my world upside down and now you need to explain it before I have a panic attack or throw a fit like a child."

If this weren't such a serious moment, I would cheer her on and give her a high-five. But alas, we're standing in front of a house that's for sale that we hate and professing our love for our childhood best friend.

Ridge steps forward and trails his fingers through her ponytail. "What he said was true, Nina girl. We want a relationship with you. All of us."

"But what—Why?"

"Careful," Trevor basically growls at her. "That sounded an awful lot like you're thinking bad about yourself."

I see the moment her attitude shifts. So when she whirls around on Trevor and stomps her little foot, I can't hold back my grin. I fucking love that she feels safe enough with us to let the old, sassy Nina out to tango.

There's my girl.

Chapter 35

Nina

Normally, the dominant stuff is a turn on, but right now it's bothering the crap out of me. "What I'm thinking," I begin while glaring at the Trevor, "is that it makes no sense why the four of you would want to be with me *and* share me. That just doesn't happen. *And* it would never work."

"Sure it will," Ridge interrupts. "I've been reading all about it."

This again?! "That's not real life."

"Then tell me what real life is, Nina." *Oh, he's mad.*

I hesitate and glance around. The four of them surround me, and since we parked down the road to surprise them, I can't just dive into the backseat of their truck. "Real life is ugly, Ridge. My life is riddled with scars and nightmares. I never sleep. I hate eating. Touch is hard, and when I close my eyes, I see monsters in the darkness."

They're silent for a moment too long, making me lose my nerve. "I have three guest rooms. You guys can stay with me until you go back home." *Because they will.* "Can I have the keys, please?"

I have no idea why I asked for them since, when I brush past Trevor, I steal the keys from his fingers. Their deep murmuring follows me down the road, but I can't bear to actually hear what they're saying.

Hitting the unlock button, I climb into the backseat of the truck and lean my head against the window with my chin tucked. Doors open and slam closed. Someone grabs the keys from the center console and starts the engine.

I would guess Trevor and Ridge are in the front, but I keep my eyes lowered so I don't give them the wrong idea that I'm open for conversation. They don't speak either. Not even when we pull into my driveway, and I hustle my way inside without a glance. Nobody comes to knock on my door once I lock myself in my bedroom. They don't seek me out, which I partly appreciate, but I feel like I'm crumbling on the inside and the only thing that can hold me together is them.

The truth is what they want to talk about is everything I've always dreamed of. But the sad part is I may have been able to have all four of them had I not been kidnapped and ruined for the world.

They don't deserve a broken thing like me, and it's only a matter of time before they realize that. The best thing for all of us is to get this over with as fast as possible before I get too attached. And the fastest way to accomplish our demise is by them moving in.

I'm terrified I'm already too attached to have a clean break. That's alright. I'd rather shatter time and time again than allow the guys to crack.

I was reborn in that basement and forged into a being meant to be broken.

D inner—food—isn't my favorite thing in the world, and I guess tonight we're pairing it with a ton of tension and pouty alpha males. I have half a mind to scurry back to my room, but Henry all but begged me to come sit with them when he found me freshening up the third guest bedroom.

I'm not sure when they left to get all their stuff from the hotel since I was hiding in my room for most of the day, but their bags are all moved into the rooms they chose. It's odd seeing their stuff in my space, but I'm aware of myself enough to realize that it makes me feel astronomically better to know they aren't leaving me tonight.

There's a hint of suspicion over the fact that none of them questioned my invitation to move in for a while. If it were me, I would have denied the offer over and over again since I would feel like a burden.

Maybe they just know their worth. I can't say the same thing about myself, which is why I'm currently staring at my salad like it can save me from the awkwardness.

"Nina."

Shoot. "Yeah?" I murmur, very much regretting how much I opened up earlier. Part of me is excited that I feel comfortable with the four of them, but the other part continues to remind me that being comfortable makes things complicated.

"Baby, look at me. Please," Trevor begs, but all it does is send me deeper into all my worries and sadness.

This, *this*, is why I don't try to be more than the meek girl everyone sees. What nobody knows and what I don't want them to know is that I have all the opinions I used to have. I wish, I *freaking* wish, I could say I *actually* believe there are two Ninas. The one before I was beaten and abused daily, and the one now. But that's not true in the slightest.

I'll say I'm not the same girl until someone rips the truth out of me. The truth is...I don't feel in past tense. I *love* softball. I *love* making friends. I *love* talking. *Gosh, I even love eating!* I love all the things I did when I was sixteen.

"Nina, damn it!"

I don't look at Trevor because I'm too busy finally processing who the heck I really am. The truth is sadder than the one where everyone thinks I've changed.

I haven't changed. I HAVEN'T CHANGED! I'm still here, just locked away like my body used to be. I want to be saved! I'm terrified to release who I really am, who I've always been, out of fear the truest parts of me will be beaten bloody all over again.

Chapter 36

Henry

I was worried when Nina wouldn't even pick up her fork. Now I'm fucking terrified. It's like she's lost in her thoughts, but the eerie part is her body is getting tenser by the moment.

"Trev..." I murmur, really wishing he would step in and tell us what to do. Ridge looks ready to jump across the table at her, my fiancé tries to coax her back to us with quiet words, and Trevor is staring at her intently.

A shuddering breath escapes Nina's lips and when her body goes completely lax, Trevor is up and out of his seat in a flash.

"Nina, damn it!"

Cursing, I jump up and watch as she all but tumbles into Trev's arms when he swoops in to grab her. "I got you, baby," he says.

Nina chokes out a sob that makes my heart crack as she clings to Trevor. "I haven't changed."

I barely hear the words she whimpers into his scruffy throat. Palming the back of her head, Trevor stands and carries

155

her to the couch. Without letting go of Nina, he curls into the corner of the sectional and motions for us to sit close.

Kai and I settle on both sides of him and Ridge takes the floor so he can hold on to Nina's ankle. With a kiss on the top of her foot, Ridge snuggles in, but I can tell he's panicking quite a bit.

None of us like our girl feeling any amount of distress, but Ridge has a certain level of anxiety that I can't relate to. I'm feeling a coiled sensation of anticipation in my gut and my heart is pounding because I just *know* this might be one of the most important moments of our lives.

"What did you mean, baby?" Trevor pets the top of her head. "You haven't changed how?"

Her brown hair falls in waves down her back and I feel compelled to run my fingers through it too. With her seated on Trevor, she looks so damn small I want to wrap her up in a blanket. Twisting around, I grab her favorite blanket with fringes and tuck her in.

Sniffling, she glances at me with big, grey eyes and I swear my heart stops at the depth of her gaze. I think her soul is shining back at me because I see the girl I've always loved.

Thirteen-year-old Nina stomping her foot at us in the cafeteria when Ridge would tease her for her dirty shoes. Fourteen-year-old Nina in a dress on Easter, begging to be the one to hide the eggs for her cousins, then coming back inside muddy and sweaty. I see the sixteen and twenty-year-old Nina staring back at me too, begging for me to *see* them.

This is what she meant. Every single piece of the girl we once knew is in there, reaching out with all her might. She just needs us to grab her hand and yank her into the light.

"Hi, pretty girl. I missed you," I breathe and run my thumb over her rosy cheeks. "I see you in there, so why don't you tell me what it is you really need to say, hm?"

I can feel the guys' confusion, but I pay them no mind. They know I've always been different...a bit more intuitive than would be considered normal. My focus isn't explaining myself, but coaxing Nina to come forward and allow herself to shine like she so desperately craves.

"I..." Her bottom lip trembles, but she stays relaxed against Trevor's wide chest. "I still like softball," she whispers and blushes.

"Me too." I beam and tickle her cheek some more. *Damn, she's gorgeous.* "What else do you still enjoy?"

Her lips twist, but after a deep breath she relents. "Going outside. Playing games. Being with you guys."

Ridge twists around on his knees so he can take her in. "What else, Nina girl?"

At that she shrugs and drops her gaze to her lap where she begins to twist the strings of the blanket around in her fingers. "E-everything." In a voice so soft she gives us the deepest part of her soul, "I'm still me. I'm just...afraid."

Kai grunts and wipes his hand over his face. It's a sure sign that his emotions are getting the best of him. Tearing my gaze away from him, I tug on a lock of Nina's hair to get her to look at me. "Afraid of what?"

The look she gives me will be one seared into my memory forever. It's a look of pure anguish and absolute need to be helped. "Everything."

"Gonna need you to give me some more, baby girl," Trevor rumbles, tightening his hold around her waist.

She wiggles as if she's shaking herself out of the trance she was in. "What if...What if I get all of myself back, only to be broken again? Even if we piece me back together, I'll be even more fragile than I ever was before. I don't know if I'll survive another shattering."

I open my mouth to reassure her we won't let anything hurt

her ever again, but she cuts me off with an angry little growl. "And what about this relationship you're proposing? It's only a matter of time before you leave me and I'll be left to pick up the pieces once you go home."

"Nina," Kai interjects, "In what fucking world do you think we would leave you? Henry and I were just house hunting so we could be as close to you as possible."

"You'll leave," Nina says adamantly, sitting up as much as possible no Trevor's lap. "There's no repairing me, Kai. Don't you get that?! Nobody wants someone in pieces."

Ridge stands and his hand darts for her chin, making her flinch, but it doesn't deter him. "If you're made of broken pieces, then we can divvy them up, you stubborn, beautiful girl. You are perfect for sharing, Nina, and we *will* be keeping you forever."

Then, to my utter fucking shock, Ridge slams his mouth against hers, claiming her for the family we are meant to be.

Chapter 37

Nina

Shock isn't a strong enough word to describe my feelings when Ridge's mouth collides with mine. My immediate reaction causes a ripple effect I think is going to change the trajectory of my life. *I gasp.*

Ridge takes my parted lips as an invitation and dips his tongue into mouth. The heat of his tongue coaxing mine out to play makes my toes curl and a flutter pulse through my core. Inside, I'm a mess of nerves and absolute excitement. I've dreamed of this moment, but I told myself it would never happen. *My first kiss.*

Hands tighten on my waist, making me moan, then Ridge digs his fingers into my scalp to position me exactly where he needs me. Someone curses, but I'm too lost in my attempt to explore his mouth. I fail spectacularly because if one thing is for certain, Ridge is in absolute control and he is *devouring* me. All I can do is grab the back of his neck and hold on tight. *I don't ever want to let go.*

My back vibrates, and the fingers near my hips burn a path

into the top of my waistband. Tingles race across my skin until I'm a whimpering mess of wiggles.

Warmth engulfs my neck. "Fuck baby," Trevor groans and I realize it was him that was vibrating. "We need to stop."

But he doesn't stop. With Ridge nibbling on my lips and Trevor's tongue on my pulse point, I'm about to unravel. I release a breathy cry when Ridge suddenly pulls away from me with a look of immense pain. His hands shift from behind my head to my jaw as Trevor moves back as well.

I *ache*. How could they stop? "Come back," I plead, knowing I sound needy, but I don't ever want him to let me go.

"Fuck, Nina. That was better than I ever imagined," he rumbles with his thumb tugging on my bottom lip.

We're both panting heavily and I'm close to begging him to kiss me again when his words finally register. My tummy flips. "You've imagined kissing me?"

Ridge frowns, but his eyes soften as he studies me. "You haven't been listening." He's so close I can smell his woodsy cologne. "Listen to me."

A lock of hair being tugged near my temple draws my attention to Henry who looks ready to eat me alive. "Hi," I say, smiling at him.

He beams and doesn't look perturbed at all by Ridge's hands still holding my face. "Hi, pretty girl."

Kai sighs something like, "so damn cute," but I'm now lost in Henry's grin. Trevor grunts in response to Kai and tugs me further into his chest. I melt and hope Ridge stays where he is. If I spent the rest of my moments like this, I would be so happy.

I think I might be kiss drunk. Everything feels a little fuzzy, and my body is buzzing with pent up energy that only adds to the ache between my thighs.

"Listen now," Henry demands softly and nods his head to Ridge.

When I turn my focus back to Ridge, I notice his glasses lower than normal. As if it's second nature, I tug his face forward and nudge his frames back up with my nose. His breath stutters against my mouth, and I only hesitate for a brief moment before I initiate another kiss. This one's softer but no less filled with desire.

"Fuck," Ridge huffs and pecks me one final time. "That's not listening, naughty girl."

Releasing his neck, I pout with a small smile. "Sorry."

His eyes narrow, as if he's trying to figure out if I'm actually upset. "Nina," he starts again, leaning back and releasing my jaw. I miss the heat of his hands immediately. "We have all dreamed of kissing you. I bet they're all counting down the seconds until they can. So when I tell you we've been in love with you for forever, I need you to try to believe me."

I open my mouth to deny his claim, but he shushes me with a finger to my lips. "No. You're listening, remember? We love every version of you, and it gives me so much joy to know those younger parts of you are still in there. And you know what?"

I hum in question, hanging on to his every word because I want to believe him so freaking bad. I really, *really* do. What makes it easier is being surrounded by the four of them this time as they say it. Every one of my senses is consumed with *them*.

Their cologne swirls provocatively in my nose. The minty taste of Ridge still lingers on my tongue and their hands haven't stopped touching me. Everything I am right now is because of them. I'm relaxed, feeling floaty, and dare I say it...loved.

Ridge says exactly what I need to hear. "We are the perfect people to coax the younger, playful Nina out."

My eyes burn because he's right. Ridge, Kai, Henry, and Trevor are exactly who I need to encourage me to live again. I think I'm finally ready.

So I take the leap and ask for their help. "Please."

Chapter 38

Trevor

This is a moment I should be ecstatic about, yet all I can focus on is the sweat dripping down my woman's forehead because she's too damn stubborn to put some fucking shorts on. Nina brushed me off when I suggested the leggings and long sleeve shirt would be too much out in the heat.

Her denial irked me less than the fact that she left her water bottle in the kitchen. I could kick Kai's ass for rushing her out the back door like a puppy with a ball. *Literally.*

The two of them have been playing catch with matching mitts and a softball for almost a half hour now, and I'm trying really hard not to put an end to their fun. But she's not even dressed for leisure activity out in Utah's June heat. *She's overheating.*

I *am* excited to see her doing the things she used to, and enjoying herself. Even if she's a bit out of practice, Nina still has a damn good arm. I'd love to see her with a baseball bat again someday. If she keeps on eating more and exercising, she will be ready to kick our asses again in no time.

My mind starts to wander while I watch my friend and our girl play. I really need to figure out what our plan is in the months to come. Delegating isn't my style, but my teams have been handling the shift very well this past month and a half. Ridge and I need to sit down with our managers, then actually come up with a long-term plan.

There's also the matter of our house and all of our shit. Henry needs his book stuff and a clean space to work. All of Kai's vlogging and hiking equipment is still at home.

We've been living out of the suitcases we stuffed full and while buying new clothes has been fun for Kai and Ridge, I really need my stuff. Unpacking in Nina's home feels like a dream come true to live under the same roof, but I worry she won't let us stay forever. *I never want to leave.*

It's been two days since Ridge made out with Nina on my lap, and my boner is becoming a fucking problem that my hand hasn't been able to fix. I'm hornier than ever seeing Nina really coming out of her shell. Her slight attitude doesn't help either, and while my hand itches to spank her, I refuse to lay a hand on her like—

"Shoot, hold on! I have sweat in my eye." Nina holds her gloved hand up to stop Kai from throwing the ball back and rubs her eye with the other.

That's it. Jumping up from the patio chair, I toss my phone on the table and stomp over to Nina. "That's enough," I growl, marching my way to her.

With her hand still rubbing her eye, she turns to me with a furrowed brow. "I don't want to stop."

Fuck, she's beautiful. I allow myself one second to drool over her slick skin and imagine licking the drop of sweat that's rolling down her throat. My dick throbs in my shorts, serving as a reminder that I need to start thinking with my other head.

My hand grabs for Nina's shirt and I give her a big tug,

forcing her to stumble into me. Nina is an average height for a woman, but having her head only coming up to my chest makes me feel like a damn king. A feral king. *I protect,* my base instincts scream and right now that means getting her out of her fucking clothes.

"Trev," she gasps as her arms fling out to rest against my pecs. Her eyeball is red from the salt and furious rubbing she was doing. "What are you doing?"

I see Kai coming over out of the corner of my eye, but pay him no mind. Honestly, I'm glad he's here. It makes me feel better knowing he's watching Nina's reaction to my caveman behavior. I'll admit, I'm terrified my dominant tendencies will remind her of that fucking monster.

"You can keep playing after you change into something more appropriate for the weather."

Her lips drop into a pout as if she doesn't realize she's playing with fire. "I'm fine."

Without further thought, I grab her hips and hoist her over my shoulder. She gasps and screeches as her ponytail whips me in the face before her hands push up on my lower back. "Trevor!"

"No, no," Kai tsks, coming closer. "If I've learned anything in my twenty-two years, it's that when someone says they're *fine,* they most certainly are *not fine.*"

She huffs and kicks her legs. My entire body locks up tight when Kai retaliates with a swat on her ass. "Nina," he scolds and moves around me to look into her face. "We've seen some of your scars already. Whatever you're hiding won't change how we love you."

"But—"

"No buts," I interject and start the short trek back to the house. I need to get her out of the sun and with the blood rushing to her head, I'm worried she's going to get dizzy. "You asked for help, baby." I remind her and walk through the back door. The chill of the air conditioning eases some of my worries.

She's silent against my back until we pass by the kitchen. "I'm thirsty," she murmurs.

I can't help myself; I run my hand up her thigh soothingly. "Good girl, Nina. Kai, grab her water bottle, please!" I yell over my shoulder as I climb the stairs.

"Oh god. Don't drop me," Nina gasps, her hands clutching my hips like a lifeline. "Omg. You are never allowed to carry me up the stairs like this ever again."

I tighten my hold on her and smile. "I won't ever drop you, baby girl. *Never*." Truer words have never been said.

Chapter 39

Nina

"Trevor?" My lip wobbles and I can't look him in the eye. Choosing to stare at my pair of black shorts and green tank top in his hands is easier. I don't want to see his first reaction to my scars. Sure they've seen my feet and bite on my calf, but what he's about to see?

"Yeah, baby girl?"

I'd like to tell him to look away and shield his eyes from the worst of my body, but this is my moment to lay it all out there. Their heated looks have ramped up in the past few days since I've begun sharing kisses with Ridge, and I really don't want our first sexual encounters to be ruined by my past.

Should I ask Trevor to watch? Then he'll see my butt, thighs, back, shoulders, and arms. The worst would be over. *But I'd have to redo this another three times.*

"Nina, look at me."

"You say that a lot," I grumble and force myself to look up at him.

He plopped me on my feet in front of my body mirror as soon as he got us safe and sound in my room. Kai tossed Trev my water bottle and closed the bedroom door to give us privacy. I swear my heart was about to thud straight out of my chest and tumble all the way down those steep freaking stairs on the way up here.

Finally, I meet Trev's intense blue eyes. My breath catches when he steps into my bubble. "And I'll keep saying it until you feel comfortable looking at me all on your own. Now..." He bends so his face is aligned with mine. "Tell me what's on your mind."

I nibble on the inside of my cheek and fight the urge to look away. Similarly, I refrain from running my fingers through his dirty blond beard. I'm afraid if I do, I'll melt into a puddle of goo at his feet.

This is supposed to be a horribly terrifying moment for me, yet all I want to do is kiss Trevor. His lips look so firm. *Would they soften if I lick them?* Maybe I could soothe the permanent scowl he's suffered with since he was a boy. To my utter horror, he reads my freaking mind!

"Nina," Trev growls, "I'll kiss your lips swollen *after* you tell me." When I open my mouth in shock, he chuckles this rumbly sound that goes straight to my vagina. "You were staring at my mouth like you were going to eat it. Now tell me."

Shoot, his tone is no nonsense. Time to make a choice. Do I rip the Band-Aid off all at once or do I share this with one and ask him to help me explain?

Taking a step back from Trevor, I grab the hem of my long sleeve. "I-I need to show you all of it. But...could you help me with-with the others?"

His brows furrow and his lips turn down. "Help you with them how?"

"I—" I suck in a breath and force myself to look him in the eye while I face my fears. "He whipped me. A lot. With belts, ropes, anything really. Always on the back. So my thighs, my bottom, my back...even my arms got hit."

I can't read the look in his eye but my heart, which I thought was going to fall down the stairs a bit ago, is now firmly lodged in my throat. Who knows what he sees in my face, but his expression settles and he nods. "How can I help?"

Blowing out a breath, I lift my shirt in preparation. "Can you just warn them that I'm not...I'm not...."

"Nina, I swear to fucking Christ if you say anything bad about yourself, I will throw you over my knee this time."

My cheeks flush and my other cheeks clench...*Is he threatening to spank me?! And why did that just send a thrill of pleasure through my veins?!*

He quirks a brow. "Did my sweet Neen like the idea of getting her ass spanked?"

I say nothing, but I know my face is saying it all for me.

Trevor hums, his eyes like molten lava as he studies me for a beat longer. "I'll give them a heads up, okay?" I nod, grateful. "Good. Turn around and let me help you."

Inch by inch, he lifts my shirt. When my arms rise above my head, I begin to tremble with nerves and fear for how things might change. Fighting every submissive instinct in my body, I make myself watch Trevor in the mirror as he catalogues every white puckered line on my body.

Whether I'm blocking out the expression on his face to keep myself safe, or he's completely stoic, I can't tell. But when his hot fingers trace a path down my spine, I shiver involuntarily.

I want to cuddle under my comforter and never leave. *Gosh, how can he look at me?*

"Breathe, baby."

At his whispered encouragement, I suck in a much needed breath. My sports bra covers most of my chest, but the silky thong he's about to see leaves nothing to the imagination. In an attempt to protect myself, I wrap my arms around my waist before I meet his questioning gaze in the mirror. I nod.

"Go ahead."

Trevor studies me for a moment before his thick fingers dig into the waistband of my leggings. My stomach revolts just thinking about what he's witnessing.

"Nina," he says my name with so much strength and emotion I can't keep myself from listening. "Breathe."

And I do. With my inhale, he yanks my pants down all the way until he's on his knees. I flush a bright shade of red when his face disappears behind my butt. Unable to deal with the sheer embarrassment of the moment, my hands fly up to cover my face.

In just my bra and panties with my pants around my ankles, I'm the most vulnerable I think I have ever been. This isn't like curling into a fetal position while kicks and punches rain down on my broken body. This is much scarier.

I'm baring myself to one of my greatest loves. Not only am I hoping he'll appreciate my thin figure, but I yearn for him to accept my pain.

Tingles race up my spine as Trevor runs a gentle finger across my butt and lower back. "You are...a warrior," he expresses with awe.

Trevor's words and warmth on the backs of my thighs unleash a choked sob from the depths of my soul. I have no response to give, only these aching convulsions pushing my deepest hurts from my body.

Pricks of pain around my hairline keep me rooted to the here and now where I *am* a warrior. My fingernails dig into my scalp as I struggle to calm myself. If Trevor would have seen me back then, lying on the cement ground in my own blood without a fight left in my body, he wouldn't think me strong.

"Beautiful." Heat presses against my hamstring with a kiss.

I breathe in his compliment.

"Strong." A tickle on my hip.

I exhale, releasing my belief of weakness.

"Stunning." His hand grabs my hip, then he's towering over me once again.

I breathe in his acceptance and drop my hands to watch what he does next.

"Courageous," he mumbles, rubbing his scruff against my marred shoulder.

I exhale my worries.

"Admirable."

I inhale, but I'm not certain I can believe that one.

"A survivor," he whispers against the top of my spine.

I exhale, making room for this new narrative he's weaving.

"Mine. Ours." Trevor wraps an arm around me and tugs me against his chest. His free hand grabs my jaw and angles my face back so our lips are an inch apart. "Say you're ours, Nina. Make me, make *us*, the luckiest men in the world."

I breathe in his request and exhale my agreement, "Yours."

Instead of taking me hard and fast like I expected him to, Trevor presses his mouth against mine so tenderly it brings tears to my eyes. The kiss is over before I can truly taste him, but by the adoration I see in his sky-blue eyes, I know this is only the beginning.

Chapter 40

Ridge

"**Y**ou gonna show her your creep cave?" Kai's teasing only serves to make me even more anxious.

"Fuck off," I grumble, shoving him up the front steps to our house. "If I'm a creep, you are too."

When Nina heard Trev and me talking about coming back to our house to get more of our shit, she asked if she could come with. I was excited to have her join us, but now I'm fucking terrified of what she'll think.

"Fair warning," Henry says to Nina, "it's a bit chaotic in there."

Trevor enters the code for the front door while I watch, fascinated, as she wraps an arm around Henry's waist and snuggles under his arm. "Four men, one house? I'm under no illusion there won't be underwear and bras everywhere."

I stiffen, annoyance rooting itself between my eyebrows. "What did you just say?" My voice is strained, but I can't help it. Nina's always undermining how important she is and always has been.

Blinking up at me with her big gray eyes, she looks nervous.

"I was joking. But even if there are bras and stuff around, I won't judge you. You're single."

"No, we are absolutely *not* single, Nina," I snap, ready to prove to her just how fucking taken I am.

Trevor slams a hand down on my shoulder. "Ridge, come inside."

"One sec," I grumble and shake him off. Without hesitating, I slide my right hand around the back of Nina's neck and get close enough to push her further into Henry.

"Ridge," she gasps. Her free hand grabs the front of my shirt, but she's not pulling away.

"If I'm not mistaken, Nina girl, you committed to be ours when you showed Trevor your hot fucking body. Did you not?" The wind picks up, swirling Nina's rose scent and Henry's cologne together in front of my nose.

"I just meant—"

My lips purse automatically. "*Just* nothing. I'm not single, I'm yours. Trevor's not single, he's yours. Kai and Henry aren't single, they're yours as much as each others."

Henry nuzzles into the other side of her neck. "I know this is all happening really fast."

I huff. We've loved this girl for far too long without acting on it. "Six years is *not* fast."

Henry glares at me through Nina's brown locks that are twirling in the wind. "And we've only reunited a few months ago, asshole." With one final narrowed look, he returns to loving on our woman between us. "This is happening, pretty girl. We love you. And no, there have been zero women in this house aside from family."

Nina visibly relaxes and presses a kiss on the inside of my arm. "Sorry," she whispers, looking sheepish.

I squeeze the back of her neck a little and give her a quick kiss on the lips. If I linger, I won't stop. "No more making what we have seem insignificant." She nods, looking thoughtful now. "Ready to see how anal Trevor is about where things go in the kitchen?"

She giggles and I swear the sun shines a little brighter.

―――――――――

K ai knocks on my doorframe and looks around my room. "Have you seen Nina?"

My heart falls out of my ass. "What do you mean?"

His brows furrow even more. "She was checking out Henry's rock collection last time I saw her."

"Well, did you ask Henry?" My mouth spits logic, but my emotions are getting trampled by *what ifs.*

Rolling his eyes, Kai starts walking away with me hot on his heels. "Obviously I would have, but I haven't seen him yet either. I figured they would both be with his books for longer than the fifteen minutes I left them alone."

Logic leaves the room right along with me. "Why the hell did you leave them alone?"

Throwing a look over his shoulder that screams *that's the stupidest thing I've ever heard*, Kai throws his hands in the air. "What the fuck do you mean, Ridge? Why *wouldn't* I let Henry and Nina nerd out over rocks and books alone?"

I bite my tongue to hold back more dumb accusations. It's not like we haven't left Nina alone. Hell, we left her every night that first month we saw her. I knew she was alone every time and was always on high alert, so now, in the safety of our home *with* one of us near her, Kai can't find her?!

I should have stayed with her.

"Ridge, we can't follow her everywhere," Kai reprimands

softly yet with every room we check and having no luck, his shoulders get tighter.

I'm about to start shouting for her when Kai throws Trevor's office door open with absolutely no finesse. "Nina?"

"What the hell?!" Trevor exclaims with a scowl. Leaning against the window behind his desk, my cousin looks ready to throttle us. "What if I was naked, assholes?"

"Then I would say get used to it, brother," Kai murmurs, but his focus is on checking the room for Nina. "We'll be seeing a lot of each other's hairy asses once we get Nina between us."

My dick perks up, not because I want to see anyone's ass except Nina's, but having her between us sounds damn good. "Speaking of, have you seen our girl?"

Trevor's features soften, and he looks out the window. "Yeah," he confirms, nodding outside.

Rushing to the window, both Kai and I take a collective breath. "Thank fuck," I murmur.

Nina and Henry are laying in the grass by the weeping willow tree. As they watch the branches sway back and forth, Henry pulls Neen closer and kisses the top of her head.

Trevor gives us an odd look. "They've been out there for a while."

"She looks happy," I whisper, not wanting to disrupt the moment.

"They both do," Kai agrees.

As if we jinxed it, the relaxed image they paint shifts into one none of us were prepared for.

Chapter 41

Nina

I'm getting little pieces of myself back every moment I spend with the guys. Curled up on the grass with Henry is one of them. "Remember all the shirts we got grass stains on?"

Henry laughs. "Yeah. My dad always asked me what kind of clouds we saw those nights I came home with green on my white shirts."

"Sometimes when I squeezed my eyes shut, I could imagine the sky. Other times I would swear I could hear your voice." I'm not sure why I feel the sudden urge to share about the worst years of my life, but I want Henry to know our memories helped me. "You saved me those days, Henry."

I feel his stare, but I keep my gaze on the sky. "There were times I never knew if I would see this again. *Feel* this again."

Shifting, he pulls me into his side. "I was terrified of never seeing or feeling you again, Nina." My throat closes over with emotion and so much heartache it's hard to breathe. "Thank you for coming home to me."

He kisses the top of my head, encouraging my emotions to

unravel a little more with tears now. My lips curve into a smile —one that's content and appreciative. "Thank you for..." I hesitate, but truly accept the words that are about to come out of my mouth. "Thank you for loving me, Henry."

"I'll love you forever, pretty girl."

The peace that was settling my constant anxiety shatters with one vicious WOOF!

All thought springs from my mind, leaving my fight, flight, or freeze instinct behind to protect me. My automatic conditioning against canines kicks in and I'm on my feet in seconds.

My neck kinks as I search wildly for the dog, but it serves as a reminder that this pain is far less than teeth puncturing flesh and muscle. "Where is it?!"

I don't sound human, and I don't hear any response. Blood roars in my ears as a shaggy gold dog runs around the decorative fence. "Stay back!" I shout, arms out in front of me as I scramble backward.

The weeping willow tree I found so mesmerizing just moments ago now blocks my vision, serving to make me defenseless against my attacker.

WOOF!

Oh my god! "STOP!"

It sprints through the yard with its tongue out and saliva swinging every which way. "Stay back!" Backpedaling like my life depends on it, I don't realize I'm close to the back of their lot until I'm tripping and falling back into prickly bushes.

A scream tears from my throat. The slices of pain on my arms and legs have nothing on the memories of a nightmare I'm reliving. *Not again, not again, NOT AGIAN! PLEASE!*

Blood running from my calf...

I have to keep running...

Run. RUN! RUN!

I can't even scream as I tumble hands first into a deep ditch that may as well be my final resting place for all the fight I have left in me.

Climb! The voice sounds familiar. Soft and throaty, enough to make me want to melt into a puddle.

"Nina!" *Henry?*

CLIMB! This voice is more frantic and energized, buzzing my insides enough to make my chin lift out of the dirt.

"Where is she?!" *I'm over here Kai!*

CLIMB, NINA! Stark fear and accusation whip through my mind, delirium making me think Ridge is standing above me and aggressively trying to beg me to move.

"WHAT THE HELL HAPPENED?!" *Help me, Ridge!*

FUCKING CLIMB! At the alpha demand of the final voice, I groan and begin to crawl.

"Shout for me, baby!"

Like that fateful day in that ditch fighting for my life, I listen to the command that sounds like my dominant man. "TREVOR!"

Chapter 42

Kai

"Take a sip, baby." Trevor tilts the glass of water, giving Nina no choice but to gulp or get soaked. "Good girl."

It hurts, physically fucking hurts to watch her trembling on Ridge's lap. His hands shake and his left knee bounces with barely restrained anxiety. He clings to our girl like if he can hold on hard enough, he can keep both himself and her from falling apart.

Witnessing Nina's pure terror when our neighbor's golden retriever waltzed into our yard is something that will stick with me forever. How many times did her eyes widen and all the blood drain from her face during those two years? The dried up blood on her skin from the bushes makes me wonder how much she's lost in her lifetime. Buckets? A fucking river? *How much goddamn blood did that monster steal from my woman?!*

"Deep breath in," Trevor coos, "and out. You too, Kai."

Hearing my name snaps me out of my downward spiral. I lock eyes with Trevor who kneels in front of Nina and Ridge on our living room rug. He mimics a deep breath and his eyes implore me to follow his lead. The breath I take feels like a shudder in my chest, but I keep at it until the twisting sensation in my gut and head is gone.

Trev nods at me and focuses his attention back on Nina who's struggling to regulate her panicked breathing. "You got it, Neen. It's just us here. Nobody's going to hurt you."

"Where is it?!" she gasps out, eyes flinging around wildly. *My god, is that what she looked like when she woke up in that hell for the first time?*

"Nina." Henry grabs her chin to get her attention. He's been gently dabbing her small cuts and dirty knees for the past few minutes since we got her inside. "Willow's owners, our neighbors, came and got her. She's not going to hurt you."

My chest clenches as I get a good look at the way her eyes are begging Henry to understand. Sitting beside her and Ridge, my fiancé uses his pinky to pet her jaw. The urge to continue pacing behind the couch is strong, but I force myself to stay in the present and try to be helpful. *How the fuck are they so calm?*

"It was coming for me!" she cries, tears streaming down her cheeks. My heart bleeds, matching every drop of her pain.

Henry shakes his head. "No, pretty girl. Willow's a goofy, fun-loving golden retriever. She was coming to say hi to us."

Nina's chin wobbles while she processes Henry's explanation. Willow really is a sweet dog. A little slobbery and thinks she's smaller than she actually is, but she's a sweetheart.

"But...Why was she running toward me l-like that?" her voice cracks along with my soul. Nina used to love dogs—all animals, really. *What happened to you, my flora?*

From my spot behind them, I watch Ridge drop his chin to her dainty shoulder and bury his nose in her neck. "Willow has an annoying amount of energy. The most she would have done is jump up on you and drown you in drool."

Ridge isn't the biggest fan of the dog next door, but I've never held it against him. There's something about Willow that overstimulates him and sends his anxiety spiking. I get it, and it's not like he's ever mean to the sweet pup. Never once has she been aggressive or bitten someone to my knowledge.

Oh fuck. My throat feels like gravel as the possibility of why she's so afraid of dogs finally sets in. "Nina, the scar on your leg..." I can't finish my thought. *It couldn't have been...*

Glancing at me, Nina looks ready to either burst into tears or throw up. I hate pressuring her to talk about the past, but I think we need to know some stuff. *Especially* her triggers. We could have prevented her panic attack had we known. That right there, not knowing and being unable to help, is what drives me to push her.

Bending so my forearms are braced on the back of the couch and our faces are a foot apart, I capture Nina's tortured gaze with my own. "What happened to your leg?"

"Kai..." Henry murmurs cautiously, but I don't break eye contact with Neen. *Does he already know?*

To my fiancé, I say, "We need to know, Hen. How can we help *before* a panic attack if we have no information?"

Annoyance flares when Trevor moves on her other side and distracts her for a moment, then he adds his own two cents. "Kai's right, baby. You need to give us *something*."

"But...why?" she whispers.

Ridge jolts back from snuggling her neck with a look of shock and rage on his face. "Why? *Why?!* 'Cause that was fucking terrifying, Nina! You went from being happy and relaxed to absolutely terrified and running for your life. Then we couldn't find you because of that goddamn overgrown tree. When we *did* find you, there was blood dripping from your arms and legs, and you were hyperventilating."

Leaning back a little to give Nina space, I wait for her to

react, but she doesn't. Cocking her head to the side, her lips twist like she's biting the inside of her cheek. Her drying eyes ping-pong all around Ridge's angry features, yet she doesn't try to leave his embrace.

Seeming to come to a conclusion, she settles deeper into Ridge's heaving chest. "I'm sorry I scared you," Nina whispers and places a gentle kiss on the edge of his mouth. "I can—I'll tell you what happened. Y-you should know, then maybe you'll understand why it's hard for me to believe you want this. Want *me*."

Ridge's jaw ticks. "Nothing you could say would ever make us want you less."

"We have always wanted you, and we always will," Trevor adds, voice thick with emotion.

Henry places a hand on her bare knee next to where he stuck a Band-Aid, and I pluck a piece of grass out of her hair. Small gestures to show we're here and we are ready to fully dive into Nina's past.

Chapter 43

Nina

I want to imagine the peace that settles over me is born of finally giving them all of me, and not numbness trying to protect me from possible rejection. I'm about to tell them about the worst moments of my life, yet aside from occasional trembles, I feel relaxed.

Whether fear has my emotions paralyzed or I truly am ready to give them my all, I can't tell, but I'm not backing down now. Even if I am disassociating a little, at least I'm not a sobbing mess anymore. Embarrassment and confusion poke at me, but I push them away in hopes of moving on from what happened outside.

Willow...such a pretty name for a creature that invoked so much fear.

"Please, baby," Trevor murmurs, grabbing one of my hands. Looking at him, I see worry in the lines around his eyes and it isn't the first time I've wondered about their lives after me. I'll ask after I unleash my horrors.

I nod softly and give him a sad smile. I'm surrounded on all sides by strong men who love me, and maybe that's why it feels like so right to open up to them. "This will be easier if I just get it all out, so please," I look around at them noting they all look a little terrified, "don't interrupt."

This is going to be hard for them, and for me, but I really do just need to power through. They exchange glances while I sniffle and grab for my glass of water. Trev narrows his eyes at me, making me pause. With a triumphant smile, he presses the cool cup to my lips. There's something about giving him control over basic things that sets me at ease.

Once I get four nods of agreement, I take a breath so deep it makes my back crack. Ridge rubs a soothing hand over my spine, and I snuggle further into him.

"So," my voice wobbles, forcing me to think about the possible consequences of what I'm about to do. "I'm going to keep this vague enough that I don't panic, okay?"

"Whatever you need, flora," Kai soothes, running his fingers through the hair on top of my head. Whether it's the use of my childhood nickname or the caress of his strong fingers, I feel incredibly grounded for what I'm about to relive.

As if my body instinctually reacts to the upcoming stressor, my eyesight blurs and my mouth turns down in forced relaxation. "After I left Ridge's house, I was pretty excited for a long walk home before the party. I thought of it like some good quiet time before my sweet sixteen and did some good thinking before..."

I clear my throat and don't dare to look up from my lap. A large part of me is worried they're only here with me now because of misplaced guilt. Kind of like my fear that my parents are obligated to put up with all my issues since I'm their daughter.

"I didn't hear the car coming, but sometimes I remember the slight squeak of the brakes that finally alerted me to someone driving by. Except he didn't drive by, and I was lost in my head thinking about—" Unbidden, my gaze flicks up and finds each of the men before flashing back down. "Doesn't matter."

I was thinking about how the past year I was starting to feel things, things my mom told me were normal for my age, but scary nonetheless, especially because I was feeling that way for *four* boys. Slut shaming and push-up bras were becoming a thing in my grade, so the insecurities were dang high.

"Anyway," I grit out, knowing the next part I'll need to skim over a bit for their sakes. "He used some force, then the next thing I knew I was in the trunk of a car and zero light was shining in."

I remember hating myself for feeling thankful for being stashed in the trunk. All that space meant that Mr. M couldn't fit in there with me. "We stopped a few times, in the middle of nowhere, to teach me a lesson about crying."

Even though I preferred the safety of the trunk, I couldn't stop the sobs from exploding from my throat. I can still feel the punch to my cheek that knocked me out, and I'm definitely still disgusted with myself for how relieved I felt when I woke up in the trunk *again*.

"I hoped and prayed I could stay in the trunk forever because I knew...I knew once he dragged me out of that small space that my life would be over. And it was." My words are nothing but a whisper as my thoughts slip free before I can get a handle on the things they don't need to hear.

Strangled noises snap me out of it and I quickly continue, hoping what I say next will make them forget my horrible thoughts. "Anyway, one of the times I woke up was in a basement. Moldy, damp, and cold all the time. I had a mattress and a..." *A bucket.*

"A what?" Henry whispers, but my ears pop and all I hear is

my heartbeat. My skin tingles and I feel myself beginning to ignore the secure pressure of Ridge wrapped around me.

My throat feels raw, and I'm not sure how long I ignore Henry's unwelcome questioning, but I pick up where it matters. They don't need to know I took care of my most basic needs in a bucket that was emptied once a week. *Mr. M would get so angry at the smell...*

"I cooked him every meal and got a few handfuls of food a week to keep me going. I cleaned the main level daily..." My palms feel the pressure of scrubbing the floor and my back flexes at the reminder of all the lashings I got. "Sometimes I had to crawl backwards so I could mop my blood on the way to the stairs."

No! Squeezing my eyes shut, I scold myself for letting that bit of information slip. I don't want to give them too much information because that would mean more questions. And I never want them knowing how weak I was to accept that monster's help every time he offered to clean my wounds. Wounds that he inflicted.

I was strong enough to cook and clean while starved, dehydrated, and beaten bloody, but I wasn't strong enough to take the out he gave me every time he *offered* to help me heal. I should have denied the stitches and cleanings...but I didn't.

So... "That was my hell for two years." *Because it wasn't life.* Being here, with my guys, *that's* life.

"And the fear of dogs?" Ridge rumbles in my ear and I can't help the shiver that zaps through my limbs.

This is almost as hard to talk about. I glance at Henry, glad one of them already knows. "The day I escaped...Mr. M was super drunk."

My natural response was to go back down to the basement, but after an hour I finally came to my senses.

"It was the opening I needed. But I didn't know about the

thing he kept chained up outside the back door." Because I hadn't been outside in years. "I was clumsy..." Malnourished and completely weak. "When I ran, it was asleep, thankfully. But my feet were heavy and during my last few steps, it...it took a chunk out of my leg."

I tune out three horrified gasps.

"He trained me not to make too much noise." *Cringe.* "But that thing was the loudest alarm I have ever heard. I ran, ignoring the pain, like I was forced to learn, then ran and ran and ran until I collapsed."

Until I heard your voices urging me onto that road.

Even if they leave me now, I will love them forever because they boosted my hope enough to survive. "I saved myself, but the love back home was my encouragement."

Just as they are now. My encouragement not only to survive but to *live.*

Chapter 44

Henry

No response would ever take away the pain my girl has suffered. So when she asks us not to say anything, I selfishly release a sigh of relief.

Ridge is frozen, his arms limp around Nina, allowing her to crawl off his lap without much effort. "I'm gonna go to the bathroom."

Then Neen's padding away with her arms wrapped around her waist. Her sniffles grow quieter as she finds the bathroom down the hall. My heart is in my goddamn throat, and I desperately want to chase after her, then never let her out of my sight.

I hate myself for how relieved I am that I didn't have to hear the details of what she suffered. *How am I so incredibly selfish and weak that I can't hold on to some of her trauma?*

The backs of my eyes sting and my head falls forward into my shaking hands. *I can't handle this.* Between the horrible relief and my brain filling in the gaps that she left open, I feel like I'm about to crumble. *Imagine how Nina feels.*

"Baby..." Kai's voice is rough, but his hands are gentle as he settles behind me on the couch and holds my hips. "She's safe now."

I lift my head and nod, but that doesn't stop the anxiety thrumming through my veins. "He's still out there. Why the hell isn't she in witness protection?!"

"I talked to her dad about that," Trevor states. "The psych facility she was in for the first year was heavily guarded, and they had frequent contact with the agents on her case when she first came home."

"What about *now*?" Ridge snaps, clearly agitated and struggling to control himself. "What's stopping him from coming after her again?"

Trev shushes him. "Calm down, Ridge. She doesn't need to hear us bickering right now."

"Continue, please," I beg, needing to know there's *something* in place to keep her safe.

"Mr. M is being tracked along the Canadian border. All signs point to him being far away from here. He's just damn good at staying two steps ahead of the Feds." Trevor's jaw clenches in irritation.

With one hand on my hip, Kai tugs me back until I'm pressed against him. "So what are they doing to keep Nina safe?" he asks, sounding more curious than angry.

Trevor scratches his stubbly jaw. "Keeping her dad updated and ensuring she's somewhat hidden. Will and Meg were terrified to shove her into hiding after everything she went through, so they felt, if Mr. M was states away, she should live her life. I don't know if any of you have thought about the fact that we never saw any news coverage of when Nina was found?"

Our beat of silence is his answer. There's a reason we never knew she was safe, and I'm pissed I haven't thought to ask before now.

"Will said there was a major uproar about it for a few days, but they quickly got it under control in an attempt to keep her as hidden as possible while she recovered. If you search the internet hard enough, you'll find her story..." Trevor trails off, suddenly looking pale.

My breath catches. "You read it didn't—"

Nina bounces into the living room with a White Claw in her hands. "I want to hear more about you guys," she says and parks her ass on the ground in the middle of the living room.

"Hold that thought." Ridge jumps from the couch and disappears.

In the twenty seconds he's gone, the three of us study Nina. Her eyes are red and puffy, yet her lips are curved up in a smile. "Pretty girl, are you alright?"

Her smile loses some of its shine. "I'm fine, Henry. I really just want to enjoy the rest of the night before we go home. As long as..." She gulps and fiddles with the can. "As long as you still want me."

"Nothing's changed," Ridge declares, charging into the living room with a stack of blankets and pillows. "And we aren't leaving tonight. So make a nest for all of us, please."

"A nest?" Kai mutters in my ear.

Nina's eyes light up and she makes grabby hands for the pile Ridge carries. With a shit-eating grin, he drops them in front of her and leaves again. Confused, Kai, Trev, and I watch as she takes a gulp of her drink and places it on the coffee table. Digging through the fabric, she hums and starts laying them around the living room.

Before I can question what she's doing, Ridge is back with more blankets and some pillows this time. Placing them on the outskirts of the scattered blankets, Ridge smiles softly and walks out again.

"Do you know what's happening?" Trevor mumbles to me and Kai.

I shake my head and lean forward. There's a weightlessness in her concentration that sets me at ease. The living room soon has a layer of blankets over the rug and pillows start to pile up in a U around the outskirts.

"Omegas in the books she reads make nests to relax in. It helps with stress and relaxation," Ridge explains, dropping more pillows on the ground. He leans against the couch, watching our girl make a cozy-looking bed. "I read some of them, and it sounded like something she would enjoy."

We're all looking at him like he has two heads, but not once does he look in our direction. Instead of questioning him, we watch Nina make the perfect spot for our slumber party.

Ten minutes later, Neen smiles and wipes her brow, then downs the rest of her White Claw. "Okay," she says triumphantly, "come snuggle and tell me all about what you guys have been up to the past few years."

Chapter 45

Nina

J ust as I did to them, they hold back some details as they tell me about their lives. I could tell they were worried about how I would react when they told me about their college experience.

A sad little voice in my head kept reminding me how much I missed out on, but I shoved it away as much as possible so I could feel happiness for the lives they've lived without me.

Unfortunately, in the dim lighting and their soft snores surrounding me, the sadness comes for me. I hide my shuddering breaths in the quietness of the night and try to memorize Henry's sharp features.

The slope of his nose, plump lips and curly black hair. *He's so pretty.* It's hard to imagine he's never been with a woman— only Kai. As for the other three, those are stories I definitely don't need details of. I never want to hear about the women Kai, Trevor, and Ridge have been with.

Apparently, the only relationship that happened is the one between Kai and Henry. The other two steered clear of commitment. I'll be honest, that scared me until they admitted they couldn't move on from me. *Sex was sex,* Ridge claimed, then proceeded to declare his love for me.

When I learned of the falling out he and Trevor had with their families, I was relieved, but also felt terrible. Those people were never around, and they sure as heck didn't deserve my two incredible men. Especially after they said those awful things about Ridge's mental health struggles.

The four of them have held onto me and my memory all these years. Ridge has his tattoo, Kai is obsessed with the scent of roses, Henry has a big rock collection, and Trev wears my ring.

It's past one in the morning, and my mind is racing, which is normal, but for once I'm not alone. Having them within touching distance is making me ache not only in my heart but between my legs.

There's something about being surrounded by masculine men that I trust on a pile of blankets and pillows that makes me want to do something I've never done; take a risk. Slipping my left arm out from beneath the covers, I suck in a gulp of air.

I can do this.

My middle finger touches Henry's smooth jaw first, then my ring finger and pointer. Nerves swirl around in my belly, and I have to shift my thighs around to relieve some of the pressure.

Gosh. I've never felt this kind of throbbing *before* rubbing myself, and the only thing I've touched so far is Henry. Ever so gently, I trace my fingers from his earlobe to his chin, then I press my skin to his lips.

Henry hums, the exhale from his nose tickling my knuckles. I hold my breath in response and pull away slightly. *What am I doing?* As if pulled by a magnet, I caress the corner of his mouth with my thumb.

I'm so entranced by the plumpness of his lips that I don't

notice Henry's eyes opening until he turns his head and looks directly at me. The small light in the kitchen makes his eyes look dark, or maybe he's feeling the same thing I am.

Wiggling again, I force myself to hold his heated gaze. When I pull away, his hand shoots up and captures my wrist. The breath I was holding whooshes out in pleasure at his cool touch.

"Henry," I whisper-moan. *Touch me*, I want to beg, but fear shoves it down.

With a firm grip, he pulls me back and places a kiss on my middle finger, then my pointer and so on. When he reaches my pinky, his teeth come out to play. A gentle nip has me quietly crying out. "Henry," I repeat more urgently this time.

The tension between us is like a live wire attached to my clit. I shuffle closer to him, hoping like heck that he won't make me say the words.

"What, Nina?" he rumbles, watching me intently. I have no time to react before he's sucking my smallest digit into his warm mouth.

I choke on my drool and shuffle until I'm pressed against his side.

Movement on Henry's other side has me stiffening and still he twirls his tongue around my pinky. "Stop teasing her, baby," Kai rumbles and props himself up on his elbow. Looming over both of us, he dips to kiss Henry's bare chest.

Heat blooms from the top of my head to the tips of my tingling toes. *Is this really happening right now?!*

Kai's attention snaps to me. "Roll over and face the other way, Nina. We're going to make you feel good. I promise."

My eyes widen, and I hesitate. "But you two—"

"Are in love with each other and with you," Kai cuts me off. "And if I'm not mistaken, *you* reached out to Henry just now."

That's true. I nod sheepishly.

Kai licks Henry's nipple and smiles at me. "Are you ready for us, Nina? Want to help me teach our man how to make you feel good?"

"Yesss," I whoosh out. My panties have never been so wet.

The time for questions is over, and Kai makes it known with his next demand. "Then roll over and press that tight ass against Henry's rock solid cock."

I don't dare kick the blankets off of my over-heated body as I twist and scoot back. The extra shield is needed to keep me sane. Although, is there really anything sane about this right now?

Henry's hands might be cold, but as his body curls around my back, we become a raging fire. The blanket isn't going to last long.

"Find her waistband," Kai murmurs. Chills race across my belly when Henry's fingers trace the top of Ridge's boxers that he let me borrow for the night. "Good. Now explore."

With one hand under my head and my leg lifting to accommodate Henry's wandering touch, I begin to sink into the sensations. My sharp gasp mingles with his groan when he finds out just how wet I really am for him.

"Fuck, she's soaked." Henry sounds shocked and...hungry.

Ever so gently, he dips a finger between my folds. Squeezing my eyes shut, I tip my head back under his jaw and breathe out. There's more mumbling behind me, but I'm lost in the teasing pleasure burning me from the inside out.

Pressure against my clit instead of a soft tickle has me bucking my hips to get more of that. My eyes shoot open and a moan slips free when I see Ridge watching us with an expression so intense my toes curl.

"Please!" I gasp out, needing Henry to rub me.

"Here," Kai says, "like this." Then my waistband is pulled tighter and two fingers swirl around the spot I need them the most.

"Oh, she likes that," Ridge pants and it's his scratchy tone that makes me notice the movement beneath his blanket. He sees my attention drift. "Is this okay? Can I come with you, Nina?"

My first sexual experience and I'm learning I can't deny them anything. Kai says roll, I roll. Ridge wants to masturbate while his friends bring me to the edge? "Okay," I whisper as hands shift between my spread pussy. "Oh god..."

"Yep, right there, my love," Kai coaches his fiancé. "You're both doing so good. Keep rubbing her wet little clit, Henry."

Kill me dead. I could listen to Kai talk dirty all night long.

My hips rock faster and when something grazes my nipple over my loose sleep shirt, I cry out in ecstasy. "Yes!"

"Keep grinding on me like that and I'm going to come in my pants." Henry's voice is tense, but I don't take his words as a warning. Instead, I increase the pressure against his penis. "Fuck, fuck, fuck."

His fingers flick me faster and Kai's fingers pluck my nipple just as Ridge tosses the blanket off of him and comes with a shout. My clit throbs and my thighs tighten.

"Henry!" I screech. My grip on the pillow beneath my head tightens just as my core does. Seeing Ridge with his head thrown back and cum rolling down his thigh sends me crashing over the edge. Stars burst across my vision and my body skyrockets and zaps with thick pleasure.

Muttered curses and heavy panting slowly bring me back to earth. Darkness reminds me that my eyes are squeezed shut, but I'm too exhausted to open them. Even hearing Trevor's rough praise about how pretty I am when I come doesn't rouse me.

There's shuffling, something wiping my vagina, then another body tugging me onto a chest. Burrowing my nose into the soft fabric of his shirt, I catch a whiff of rose. *Kai.*

"Sleep now, flora. We love you."

A tough day was just the thing we needed to grow closer.

Chapter 46

Trevor

"Have you heard from Nina?" Meg sounds worried, instantly putting me on alert.

My heart pounds as my fingers flex on my phone. "No. Why? Is she not home?"

"No...She's not..."

I check the clock on my dashboard, and my gut tightens with something like dread and fear. "Kai and Henry should have picked her up twenty minutes ago. Maybe they stopped to get her a coffee."

Silence on the other end of the line doesn't make me feel better. "Trevor," Meg's voice wobbles. "I already called both of them. And Ridge. He said Nina left his house forty minutes ago. Kai got a text from her saying she was going to walk home."

"But even if she walked—" she would be home already.

"Hey man."

Glancing over my shoulder, I see Kai coming toward the patio door. "Hey."

"You alright?" He leans against the door frame and crosses his arms same as me. "You've been over here for a while."

I nod at Nina who's curled up on the couch outside. "She's still on the phone."

Kai mimics my nod but doesn't take his assessing gaze off of me. "Yeah. Meg misses her. That's not what I asked though."

The urge to brush him off is strong, but if I bury this shit, then it will come out in other ways. Ways that I fear would impact Nina. "I can't stop thinking about that day." He knows which day. "She was just...gone."

As the minutes wore on, my soul felt like it was expanding and stretching as if it was searching for her. With each hour, a new tear would form and my knees would wobble. Our search party almost brought me to my knees so many fucking times.

Then we found it; her backpack.

"Trevor. Blink, she's not going to disappear."

Self-hatred and guilt rages to the surface. "She did the last time I took my fucking eyes off of her!"

Kai raises a brow. "And yet, now you're looking at me. Not her."

My teeth are going to be nothing but dust by the time I'm thirty. Annoyed, I return my attention to my girl. "I didn't mean it literally, asshole."

"No, but you're going down a path that isn't only going to hurt you, but it's going to hurt her too."

"The fuck are you talking about?" I shoot him a look and notice how serious he looks. *Am I really coming across so poorly?*

"You look like you're ten seconds away from locking her in her bedroom." *Not a bad idea.* "No, Trev. Stop that shit right now. Nina has put in so much effort to move forward and continue living. If you let the past drag you down into a pit of anxiety, you'll take her with you."

"I'm fine." Fuck him for scolding me like a child.

"You aren't," he says matter-of-factly. "We all need a pep talk sometimes after losing the most precious thing in the world, but what we need to focus on is *she's here*. Nina's alive, in one piece, and just *look at her!*"

I am, and I don't ever want to stop. Nina's head snaps back and her twinkling laughter moves through the glass door. Admiration hits me like a brick in the chest. This woman is the epitome of strength and perseverance.

"She's smiling, laughing. We need to join her and encourage her, Trev. Take a while to center yourself again." Kai places a hand on my shoulder. "The scars will always be there, but they're a sign of the past. That," he gestures to Nina, "is our future. Don't let the trauma blind you, brother."

With those parting words, Kai leaves me to keep watch over the woman who has our hearts. *No, not watch over.*

Nina's safe, happy, healthy—even if she should still be eating more—maybe it's time to reframe the narrative.

Relaxing my stance and shaking out my shoulders, I imagine my worries fading until they're tucked away under logic. I can see with my own two eyes that Nina is alive, and each day she's closer and closer to *thriving*.

We may not have gone further in our relationship since last week's slumber party at our house, but it feels like it doesn't really matter. Rushing this is not what any of us need. If I'm being honest, I need to go slow with her.

There's so much fear banging away in my chest and mind that I need to sort out first. Maybe this conversation with Kai was the wake up call I needed. Nina has so many scars and so do we. They're different, but Nina's working so damn hard not to let hers ruin the rest of her life. I shouldn't either.

So, taking a page out of Nina's book, my lips curve into a smile.

"I f you get nervous at any point, squeeze my hand or tell me so, okay?" Fuck, *I'm* nervous. Damn Ridge and his idea of taking Nina out on a date.

It's just coffee, he said, but we all insisted that the first date should be with all of us and I admit I'm still feeling slightly anxious even after my talk with Kai yesterday.

Nibbling on the inside of her cheek, Nina looks around, then peers up at me. "Okay," she whispers, her voice cracking slightly.

"I'm about to fall over if I don't have any caffeine!" Ridge shouts, breezing by us and giving Nina a little slap on the ass.

"Ridge!" she squeals and tries to run after him with the cutest little scowl on her face, but my grip on her hand is firm.

I tsk and tug her back. "No running in the parking lot, baby girl."

Deflating slightly, Nina hangs back with me while Kai chases after Ridge, shouting about defending his woman. She rubs her ass cheek and scowls at the two idiots. "He's always doing that."

Henry snorts, coming up on her other side after locking the SUV. "I'd guess Ridge enjoys the reaction he gets from you, pretty girl."

She turns thoughtful, but as we come up to the cafe door, I

draw her attention back to me. "Nina, what are you going to do if you feel uncomfortable or want to leave?"

"Squeeze your hand if I can't say anything." She blinks up at me with a little smile that makes my heart soar. Ridge helped her get out of her head and I'm giving her a safe place to land.

I can't fucking control myself when she yields to my dominant side so beautifully. Without further thought, I bend and press my lips to hers. They part on a gasp that draws me in like a moth to a flame. My hand that's not holding hers dives into her wavy hair and I yank her into my body.

"Alright, alright..." Henry mutters, breaking the spell Nina put me under. "Easy man. How 'bout we eat her at *home*, not outside the coffee shop?"

Releasing my woman is harder than it should be, so I don't. Instead, I pepper her cheeks and jaw with kisses until I've calmed down enough. Except, when I pull back, her eyes are blown wide, and she's panting.

"Goddamn."

Groaning at the sound of Ridge's voice, I pull back. "Way to ruin the moment."

"Pretty sure that's exactly what you needed considering you're in the middle of a sidewalk on a Sunday morning," my cousin retorts and opens the door.

Nina shivers and I refuse to believe it's the whoosh of air-conditioning filtering out of the building. Instead, I choose to think it's the final kiss I give her before tugging her inside.

"Alright, flora," Kai claps, basically skipping over to the display case of pastries. "Cheese danish?"

"Oh my god!" a teenage looking boy gasps, stumbling toward us like his excitement throws him off balance. Nina stiffens beside me and takes a step back as the kid zeros in on her.

Kai steps in, placing himself between us and the unwanted attention. "Hey man, back off."

He doesn't even *look* at Kai, only Nina who has begun to shake. "You're that girl that escaped Mr. M, aren't you?!"

The teen's volume is low, but Neen hears every word. Like the stunted asshat he is, the boy doesn't read the room. "Holy shit, dude. I'm like *obsessed* with all of his cases. I can't believe they still haven't caught him. I saw the few news stories on you, but it's like everything went silent. Did you go into WISTEC or something?! That would be SO cool."

My hand cramps and spasms. The force of Nina's panic radiates through my knuckles and up my wrist. "Home. NOW!" I snap, and scoop my baby girl up into the safety of my arms.

Chapter 47

Nina

C ool. *So* cool.

That kid knows *nothing*. I have half a mind to find him and scare him straight. Initially, I was in so much shock I had no choice but to listen to the stupid words that came out of his mouth. Then, by the time I registered the awful things he was saying, I shut down.

I know I scared the guys, Trevor especially, but processing the fact that someone thinks what I went through is *cool* was a completely new situation to be in.

Henry's hand enters my line of sight with a frantic wave. "Nina, I'm going to need you to stop staring at the scissors like that, please."

Blinking, I tear my gaze away from all the sharp objects on Henry's desk. He's converted my basement into a workstation so he can continue working on restoring books and fulfilling special edition orders. I didn't hesitate to offer him the space down here considering I would never choose to spend my time in a basement ever again without one of the guys.

"Sorry," I mutter, shifting around to shake off my angry

thoughts. Trevor was getting on my nerves with the whole *drink this, eat that* mumbo jumbo, so I retreated down here to hang out with my calm Henry.

Henry eyes me and wipes down another tool. "I haven't seen you look like that since the day Ridge convinced the umpire he foul ticked the baseball and it wasn't a strike."

And just like that, my annoyance reaches for the surface. "He absolutely did *not* touch that dang ball."

Henry laughs quietly and steps between my legs where I sit on the marble counter in the mini basement kitchen. *It really is a nice space down here...*

He tucks some hair behind my ear and runs his thumb along my cheekbone. "Whatcha feeling, Nina? I expected you to retreat a little after this morning's ordeal, but this frown and steam coming out of your ears in unexpected."

My eyes roll to the ceiling and stay there. "I'm just so...so...ugh!" I throw my hands in the air and Henry catches them.

"Hey," he scolds and places my palms on his chest.

As I force myself to blow out a breath, I meet his eyes. "I'm angry and I don't know what to do about it." Anger obviously isn't a feeling I have very often. Indifference, self-pity, sadness, hopelessness. Yeah, I feel those things. "No part of what happened is *cool*! Who says that?!"

It's all bubbling and boiling now, and there's no stopping the frustrations from overflowing. "And how inappropriate to approach me like that! I was clearly panicking, and what if he triggered me? I just can't believe someone would say those things to a known victim."

"Nina, he *did* trigger you."

"No, he didn't. I'm not sobbing in a ball under the stairs." I shake my head, frowning up at Henry.

The lines between his brows soften. "There's more than one

feeling to have after being triggered. You don't get angry often, do you?" I shake my head. "You *should* be angry about how that kid treated you. That's a healthy reaction, but letting it fester until you're about to pick up my scissors isn't."

He winks, so I know he's just teasing me. "I wouldn't have done that." My protest is light and airy, just like how I'm feeling after unleashing some of the crap in my head.

"Mhmm," he hums and eyes my mouth when I wet my lips. "I'm so proud of you, Neen. I love you."

He doesn't give me a chance to respond before his mouth is on mine and I'm melting into his firm grip.

Anyone clearing their throat would have pulled me from the moment, but when a loud cough sounds through the mini kitchen and it sounds like a woman, I jump and spring from the counter. The move puts Henry behind me like I'm going to save him from my very red-faced mother.

"Mom! What-what are you doing here?" I peek back at Henry and notice he's eyeing her with a mixture of amusement and embarrassment.

She crosses her arms and cocks her hips. "Well, hello to you too, daughter. I just had a very peculiar conversation with Ridge, who is now getting the third degree from your dad."

I swear my heart scurries into its hiding spot in my throat. "What did Ridge say?"

Mom raises a brow. "I think it's time we had a chat, sweet Nina."

F or the love of everything, ever, please don't make me have this conversation with my mom. We bypass dad sitting at the kitchen table with Kai, Ridge, and Trevor looking ready to either flee or fight.

Mom doesn't even spare the man behind us a glance. "Henry, why don't you join the boys, hm?" *Oh god...* "We'll be outside having girl talk. Will, bring some wine when you're done, please?"

"Sure thing darling," Dad replies easily without taking his eyes off my guys. My face is on fire and Ridge winking at me does nothing to cool me off.

"Alright, spill," Mom demands once we're on the patio and she settles onto the couch.

Instead of sitting where she is, I start to pace. When my lip wobbles, Mom catches my forearm in a gentle grip and stops me. "Nina..." she says softly, her eyes shining with something I can't read. "Are you in love with them?"

"Yes!" I rush out, thankful she made it easy for me. I really truly do want to talk to her about this; I'm just terrified. "Are you judging me?"

"Goodness, no." She seems so startled by my question that it sets me at ease. At ease enough to finally sit next to her. "I've read some of the stuff you have on your e-reader and I always wondered."

"Oh my god, you what?!" I'm going to be sick. There's some really kinky stuff on there for when the mood arises. "Mom," I groan into my palms.

"I do see the appeal. But I really have to ask how they ended up moving in here, and if you're okay with everything going on." She plucks my hands away from my face and studies me. "I love those boys, but I need you to tell me if you're feeling pressured into anything."

The breath I release is so cleansing, I feel lighter all the way down to my pinky toe. "They've been so wonderful, Mom. We've had a few bumps and who knows what this means long term, especially because Henry and Kai are engaged, but I really do want this to work."

She's quiet and attentive as I explain how our relationship has come to be. About the conversations I've heard the guys having to keep jealousy and issues between the four of them, then keeping me out of it if they start to bicker.

"They're putting me first and ensuring that keeping my anxiety low is a priority. If there's been an issue about sharing, I haven't heard anything about it." I hadn't really thought of it until now, but I really hope that's a good thing.

"And your birth control? You said they didn't replace it, but how are you going to stay safe, Nina?" Her eyes are narrowed and the tone she uses is stern.

"We haven't had sex, Mom."

She raises a brow. "And when you do?"

"I haven't really thought about it," I admit, feeling anxious again. "It's something we'll have to talk about because my new doctor is hesitant to do anything until I'm back to a healthy weight."

"How much are you eating?"

And so the nervous lecture continues. My mom and I have always been close, but after everything that happened, then me spending an entire year isolated at home with her? We're struggling to be away from each other.

I answer her questions truthfully, with a touch of evasiveness, because she really doesn't need to know how often I wish they would touch me more.

Chapter 48

Ridge

Will is the dad I always wanted, but I have to say, saying bye to him and Meg after two days of them visiting is a relief. Thankfully, he didn't try to kill me or the guys, but there were plenty of threats.

The conversations he had with us weren't the normal *if you hurt my daughter I'll make your life hell.* No, this was much deeper than that. It felt like he was quizzing us to see how much we've learned about Nina and her triggers.

Basically, Will wanted to know if we could actually take care of her without getting frustrated with the things that make her different. Our assurances bounced off his thick skin, but eventually, our words sank in.

That doesn't mean he made our lives easier while they were here. I'm pretty sure Will didn't blink once. Whether he was staring us down or wide-eyed watching Nina play catch with me outside, he was always watching.

Meg was a little less awestruck than her husband, but she made a point to hug each of us a little longer and even whispered *thank you* in my ear a few minutes ago. Knowing Nina's parents approve of our relationship makes me feel freer.

With a deep breath, I enter my room at the back of the house and grab my sketch pad. It feels like time I share this side of me with my girl again. As I'm walking out of my room, the bare walls catch my attention. Nina has her guest rooms furnished, but there are no decorations or personal touches.

We've been a bit hesitant to lay down roots in her home since she's under the impression that this is temporary, but I feel like she needs us to take the lead and stake our claim.

Eyeing the box shoved in the corner of the room, I think about my decision for two seconds, then decide *fuck it*. I'm here to stay. I'm a permanent fixture in her life, and this is as great a way as any to show her that.

I'm sweating. Since I started this project, I haven't been able to stop. I don't even know what time it is. My shirt disappeared about half a wall ago, yet it feels like I'm outside basking in the sun. Whether it's excitement or anxiety, I can't really tell.

Truthfully, I'm worried when Nina sees what I've done in her guest bedroom she's going to think I'm a creep. I know a few ways to take her mind off of my stalker ways, though.

So when a choked inhale and a loud thud sounds behind me, I'm glad I'm already half naked. This is going to be much easier if I can distract her with my six-pack. "Nina girl," I drawl, turning around with a panty melting grin. *No, I wasn't lying when I said I was reading her books.*

Her big gray eyes widen with each sketch she comes across

—and there are *many*. One entire wall, almost floor to ceiling, has my drawings taped to it.

"Ridge." Her hand flutters up to her mouth as she slowly steps into my bedroom. "What is this?"

"I'm moving in," I joke, but all she does is glance at me like she already knew that. I clear my throat and rub my neck while Nina studies each sketch like they're gold. "They're you. A lot of you. And the guys."

"You drew us," she murmurs, sounding reverent.

"I sketch what I love."

"Ridge..." Her eyes look pained when she looks at me. "Where's the color? You did such *beautiful* color."

"My life lost its color when I lost you, Nina." Honesty feels easy because everything I have to offer revolves around her. Nina is my world. "I started working with charcoal a lot to feel closer to you." Charcoal was Nina's medium of choice.

No response is needed, and I'm content with the look of understanding and heartbreak in her gaze. *She understands.* Tears track down her cheeks as she nods. I smile and wait to see what she'll do next.

She sniffles while looking at one I made last week while she and Kai were chatting on the couch. Both were slumped against the cushions with only their heads turned towards each other while they spoke quietly.

The room is silent as she makes her way through my artwork. The next one Nina wipes a tear at is one of her and Henry snuggled up by the fire together. I wasn't able to recreate the look of pure serenity on her face.

Pointing at it, she glances at me with a little frown and watery eyes. "I don't look like this, Ridgie."

I stay where I am, not wanting to interrupt her moment. "What do you mean?"

"You made me..." She looks at it again. "Beautiful. Happy..."

Fucking hell. Screw giving her space. Closing the distance between us, I grab her jaw and tug her around to look me in the eye. "Nina, are you *not* happy?"

Watching her eyes glaze over for a moment while she thinks about her answer physically hurts me, then she gives me the tiniest of nods. "I think I am."

"Say it," I demand, needing her to own the fact that she is, in fact, *happy.*

"I'm happy," Nina mutters. I raise a brow and she giggles a little laugh. Louder this time, she announces, "I think I really am happy, Ridge."

"And beautiful," I sneak in, but she doesn't fall for it. "Don't make me tell Trev you were talking shit about yourself. I know he keeps threatening to spank you and this might just be the time he follows through on it."

Gray eyes narrow at me. "He wouldn't."

And like absolute divine intervention, Trevor walks in. "Who wouldn't what?"

"Nothing!"

"Tell me, cousin," I drawl, slowly stepping back from my girl to point at a sketch, "do you think Nina looks pretty in this one?"

Trev comes closer and takes in the image of him plopping a piece of popcorn on Nina's tongue. "Absolutely exquisite."

"And this one?" I gesture to another where she's pushing my glasses up my face with her nose.

"Beautiful," he agrees, nodding while he continues to admire all my artwork. There are so many of Nina alone that I'm shocked she hasn't called me out for being weird. "This is my favorite, though."

Trevor plucks one off the wall of just Nina. In this image, her face is canted down, but her shining eyes are looking up at me. Her waves tumble near her cheekbones, making her look innocent and sad. Her bottom lip sticks out in a little pout too, so it's no wonder that's Trev's favorite.

"I...Thank you," Nina stutters and shifts in place. When I look over, I catch her checking me out. Then she bites her lip and I can't keep myself from stepping back toward her. Snapping her gaze up to my face, her cheeks instantly redden.

"Where are Kai and Henry?" My tone is thick. Actually no, that's my cock.

"Date night," Trevor replies easily.

Humming, I take another step toward my wiggly girl. "What do you say we have our own?" I ask my cousin in a low voice that promises wonderful things for us if he agrees.

"I'd say..." Trevor rumbles and walks around me. Nina doesn't move as he edges behind her and swipes the hair from her shoulder. "That I just figured out what I want to eat."

Fuck yes.

Chapter 49

Nina

"Trev?" His name comes out sounding shaky. I *am* shaking. I'm hoping whatever's about to happen is what I haven't been able to stop thinking about. My clit pulses in agreement.

"Shh," Trevor coos in my ear. "We got you, baby. If you say stop, we'll stop, okay?"

My eyes flutter closed and I let my head fall back onto his hard chest. "Okay," I whisper, loving the feel of giving into him.

"Look at me, Nina," Ridge demands, sounding so much closer than he was. I do as he says and find him staring down at me with a look of pure fire behind his glasses. "Do you want this? Want *us*?"

Do I ever... "Yes. Please."

Trevor hums while trailing his stubble down the side of my throat. "One thing you'll never have to do with us, baby girl, is beg."

A squeak bursts from my mouth as my legs are swept out from under me. I gasp out Trev's name again and cling to his neck as he slowly lowers me onto Ridge's bed. Already feeling a little woozy with excitement and the manhandling, I tug on Trevor's shirt until he's laying on top of me.

"You feel safe in my arms?" Nothing but love shines in his watchful gaze.

His hair parts beneath my fingers like silk as I pet him. "I do." Apparently, I'm not capable of much verbal affirmations but that just goes to show how gone I am for these men. *My men.*

"Yes, Nina girl." The bed dips beside us. *"Your men,"* Ridge agrees easily. *Oops, I said that out loud.*

Trevor leans down to my ear. "How about we take some clothes off? You okay with that?"

For the first time since they soaked my panties, I hesitate but nod in the end because I trust them. I'm sure Trevor has warned them about my body enough that Ridge won't gasp and run away once he sees my backside.

I fight to keep my bottom lip from pouting when Trevor pushes himself off of me. It helps that he looks so dang yummy kneeling between my legs and—*Ope, there goes his shirt.*

"Do you ever skip the gym, man?" I giggle and notice Ridge glaring at his cousin's muscles. "You're thick as shit."

I laugh again when Trevor makes his pecs dance. "Not the only thing that's thick."

Just like that, my cheeks flare so hot I have to cover them with my hands. "Oh my gosh," I mumble into my palms.

Something hot and wet pulls on my earlobe, making me startle and lift my hands to swat it away. Trevor stops me. "Ah, ah, baby. Let my cousin have a taste of your pretty skin while I take these pesky leggings off."

"Jeez," I grumble, immediately melting into a puddle when Ridge nips and sucks on my ear. "Oh!" My butt flies off the bed when an amazing tickle on my vagina zaps through me. I feel so incredibly naïve, but I have no time to feel poorly about my lack of experience. These two are making my body sing so loud all the bad things are drowned out.

This could get addicting.

Cool air on my bare thighs is quickly replaced with Trevor's warm shoulders. "What are you—"

Then, to my complete and utter astonishment, Trev licks between my folds and groans like he just tasted the best thing ever. No words come out of my mouth as my head flings back into the pillows and my heart pounds wildly in my chest.

Warmth encompasses my cheek and tugs on me until my lips meet greedy ones. *Ridge.* "Remember to tell us to stop if you don't like or want something," he reminds me and starts nibbling on my jaw.

"Don't stop!" Diving my fingers into Trevor's hair, I tug him to me and arch my back, which Ridge takes his opening to lift my shirt and bra.

"So rosy," he mumbles, and sucks my nipple into his mouth.

I jolt at the stream of pleasure that zips through my veins and totally soaks Trevor's beard. "OH GOSH! Don't stop, don't stop!"

My belly clenches and I swear I feel my vagina pulsing, trying to find something to grab onto as the greatest orgasm of my life builds. Just as I think it's going to be all alone, Trevor shifts and something prods my entrance while Ridge sucks on my tingling chest.

"Yes! Finger me. Please Trev. Please, I need you!" I'm shouting gibberish and things I'll be embarrassed about later, but all that matters is the incredible and mind-numbing pleasure that freaking *bursts* through my body when he does as I ask.

I think...I think I'm simultaneously floating while also being held down by bone deep satisfied exhaustion. My breaths are labored, and there's a subtle rubbing on my clit still that makes me wiggle with aftershocks every now and then.

The chill almost comes for me, then something warm presses against my right side. "Sleep now, Nina girl," Ridge murmurs. "We'll take care of you."

Nothing has ever felt as good as it does to believe the promise he just gave me.

Chapter 50

Kai

"**D**o you think she's doing okay?"

Henry's question throws me off a little. He's always been the one to sense things like that. Sometimes I wonder if he has a little magic, not just in his pants, but it really feels like he's connected to something *greater*.

Trevor crosses his arms and disrupts my thoughts. "She needs more fucking sunscreen."

Henry cocks his head as if he can tell how many layers of sunscreen she has on her bare arms and legs through the glass door. I roll my eyes. "Chill, cavemen. And I think Nina's doing great, Hen. Why do you ask?"

"Don't know," he mutters, further increasing my anxiety. "She just seems like...*good*, you know?"

"No, I don't know." I frown, turning him toward me and Trevor so we can talk about this. "What's wrong with *good*?"

Running a hand through his dark curls, Henry looks flustered and a flustered Henry means it's time to give him more support. After that first year of the four of us spiraling after Nina went missing, Will sat us all down and reminded us Nina wouldn't want us losing ourselves. Since then, we've fallen into a natural habit of taking turns with big feelings. Sure, we overlap every few months, but we've learned the best ways to support each other.

With Trevor, he needs a firm hand, kind of similar to Ridge. Where Ridge needs someone to push him out of the past, Trev needs a slap of reality. I usually need a hug and someone to lean on and we have to tug Hen back to the present lest he get lost in future what ifs.

"What happens when she regresses again, like when something triggers her, because it *will* happen. The fall is going to be so far because she's so high right now."

"Baby..." I interrupt his panicked rambling with a tight hug. With my fiancé wrapped in my arms and my woman sun bathing out on her patio with more skin showing than she ever would have dared a few weeks ago, all feels right in the world. Seeing Ridge out there tickling her bare tummy gives me all the warm fuzzies that this is going to work.

"He has a point." Trevor sounds pained, and when I look over, I see him frowning pretty damn hard. "Shit, we can't let her fall."

Henry pushes back from me a few inches and gives Trev an exasperated look. "Nina's going to fall, Trevor. Everyone falls."

"I won't let her," Trev retorts with his teeth clenched and posture rigid.

Keeping an arm around Henry, I reach the other one toward Trevor and snatch his T-shirt. With a hard yank, he stumbles into us with a curse and some choice words about my asshole.

"Hush," I tease and wrestle him under my arm so the three of us are in a small huddle. "Stop being all *daddy* and listen to what I have to say."

Henry chuckles and quickly hides his smirk when the big

guy glares at him. To me, he snarls, "Don't *ever* call me that again."

"Yes sir," I nod enthusiastically and bow my head. Henry laughs again, making me feel like a king.

"Kai," Trevor warns, but he's not fighting our little three-way hug anymore.

"Calm down," I groan and give him a squeeze before releasing all that muscle. I keep Henry tucked close to my side as I give Trevor the reality check he needs. "Nina's going to fall, just like we do. But we'll be there to help her catch herself. She's strong—"

"The strongest," Trevor agrees softly, his eyes trailing back to Nina currently getting peppered with kisses by Ridge.

I glance at Henry and notice he's also hanging onto my every word. "We're here to lighten the load, not lift her up. Neen has proven time and time again that she can stand on her own. So when she falls, we'll remind her just how capable she is and encourage her to stand again."

My nose leads me to the kitchen and when I see Nina wiggling her hips in front of the stove, my dick propels me forward. Burying my nose in the crook between her shoulder and neck, I relish in her throaty gasp. "Whatcha making, miss flora?"

"It's a surprise, fauna." She bounces on her toes, and I swear to fuck I'm going to come in my pants.

Groaning, I kiss her neck. "Keep wiggling your hips like that and *you're* going to get a surprise." Throwing caution to the wind, I grind my erection into her pert ass.

"Kai!" Nina's left hand flies up to grab the microwave. "Hot. The stove is hot."

Pulling my weight off of her, I panic. "Shit!" I pick her up and swing her around until her ass is on the *cold* island. "Are you okay? I'm so sorry, I wasn't thinking."

Fuck, I'm such an idiot. I see no injuries, or burn marks, but that doesn't mean I didn't scare her. *How could I be so stupid?!*

"Hey." The hand not holding the ladle touches my cheek, drawing my attention to her pink cheeks and searching gaze. "I'm okay."

My eyes narrow on her obviously heated flesh. "You're red."

"I uh—" Nina shifts and glances down. "I'm embarrassed."

"What?" *The hell is she talking about? I almost burned her.* "Nina, I almost hurt you and you're embarrassed?"

"Um." She wiggles again and I have half a mind to pull her leggings down to make sure she didn't burn her hips. Then she blurts out a statement that wakes my dick back up. "I liked it! It-it turned me on."

I open my mouth with a smirk, ready to tease her and maybe tease an orgasm out of her. But the ladle presses against my lips, effectively cutting me off.

"Shoot, I hope that wasn't hot." I shake my head in answer to her worry. "Phew. Okay, no, just don't say anything. Let me finish making you dinner while you hang with the guys outside, please? Just ignore that, or you know...maybe we can try again later, but I have a timer on and it's really important—"

"Okay, flora," I cut off her cute rambling and seal it with a scorching kiss before helping her off the countertop. "I'll see you and your surprise in a bit."

With a wink and a kinky promise, I leave her to it.

Chapter 51

Nina

The longer I've been gone, the more my worry worsens. I just *know* the guys, or at least Trevor will be mad that I left without saying anything. Well, that's not true. I *did*. I left a little note on the counter saying I needed to run to the store quickly.

Since I've been doing so well, I felt like this was the perfect opportunity for me to prove to myself that I can be an independent woman that didn't freak out in public. I bet I'll be back in time before they notice.

The first half seems to be true, but I'm getting closer to an anxiety attack with each passing second it takes for the cashier to ring up the lady ahead of me.

I had forgotten peanuts in my grocery order this week and what I'm making for dinner *needs* roasted peanuts to it pull it all together. This is the first meal I'm making them, so it has to be perfect. And peanuts will make it perfect.

So here I am, waiting in line at the gas station a few minutes away from home, clutching a jar of peanuts like my life depends on it. Just when I think it can't get any worse, it's my turn to check out and I swear I completely disassociate.

Gosh, I hope I paid correctly, I think to myself as I rush back to my car. Thankfully, the hard part is over and I can get back home to the guys.

A smile stretches my lips as I recall their boyish laughter out by the fire. With beers in their hands and heads thrown back, I felt such a rush of love that there was no way I could have interrupted their moment.

I'm afraid they'll realize I'm too much of a burden for them, which is part of the reason I've been white knuckling my newfound happiness like it's the only thing connecting me to them. I know it's not true, but it also feels good to feel...well, *good*.

I've spent so long suffering in silence, it's amazing to release the little girl I used to be and play. I've laughed so much these past three or four months amongst some tough moments of panic that I feel like maybe, just maybe, I can live a normal life.

So yes, I left by myself to get peanuts without verbally saying anything because they deserve their own little slice of heaven too, which I'm pretty sure is what I witnessed right before I left.

Rounding the neighboring car, I pull my keys from my sweatshirt pocket—yes, I'm still self-conscious—and flip it around to find the unlock button. I reach for the handle just as I hit the button but stop when movement on the other side of the hood draws my attention.

Life stalls.

My heart stops beating.

And my soul backpedals into a dark, safe trunk where the world won't hurt it. Where *he* can't hurt it.

Except, it's not just my soul that stumbles backward, my

feet do too. My hope for a beautiful life isn't the only thing to crash and crack open to bleed.

"No. No. No!" With each heart shattering plea for the universe not to do this to me a second time, I step back. Then another, and another, until I'm so twisted up inside that my feet follow suit, then send me crashing to the ground.

Pain slams through the back of my head with a resounding *boom*, jarring my teeth and plummeting me into a pit of darkness that doesn't feel safe. Because while my mind is blacking out with the agony of cracking my skull on the curb, my body is left at his mercy.

Mr. M found me.

Coming Soon
Part 2 Coming July 15th, 2025!

Damaged Duet
~MMFMM
~Hurt/Comfort
~Triggers

Coming This Fall
Wilted Duet

Petals of Blue
Part 1 & 2
~MMFMM
~Grovel
~Badass FMC

Also by Y.V. Larson

Always With You duet
(Completed)
A dark, emotional MMFMM romance
Never Moving On
Never Losing Hope

Wherever We Go series
A series of interconnected single mom MMMMF standalones
Just You & Me
Simply You & Me
Utterly You & Me (TBD)

Collapse of the Premuim Designation series:

The Invisible Omega duet
A dark, emotional academy MMFMM Omegaverse
Met Your Match
Met Your Mate

Acknowledgments

First and foremost, I need to say thank you to my husband for being my biggest cheerleader! When I started this journey a few years ago, I never would have thought I'd be here, yet he never once doubted me. Sometimes he has even been far more excited about my accomplishments than me! I'm so thankful for his support and encouragement.

When I first started writing, I was worried about how my friends and family would react to my genre of choice. All the people supporting me and cheering me on have pleasantly surprised me. Many of my family members have even read some of my work *blush*. Thank you to my parents and in-laws for not judging me or frowning at my work. It means the world to me that I can share my dream with the people I love the most.

ALPHAS! Angelica... Patricia... Brandi... Kassandra...you got me through some moments of uncertainty. The hype you ladies have given me has been beyond my wildest dreams! Your kind words and helpful critiques left me feeling proud of my work. Thank you from the bottom of my heart!

BETA BESTIES! Salima, Melissa, Leanne, Reina, Alanys, and Renee ... our group chat ended up being far more than updates. I am truly so grateful for your friendships and your motivational help!

Scarlett, my editor! You are amazing. I have no idea how

you do it, but I am in awe and so thankful for the effort and work you put into this story. Thank you!

S.E. Green, my book bestie! I feel like I need to say thank you for so many things. For everyone reading this, S.E. is literally everything. Thank you for keeping me sane, reading all my random snippets, calming me down when I get a bad review, being my cheerleader, teaching me all the techy things, etc. I could keep going! Thank you for being so amazing all the time.

READERS! You all blow my mind. Thank you for all the kind words you have given and for taking the time to allow my stories to take up a little portion of your day. I write what I love to read, and I'm so honored to have a space in your libraries.

About the Author

There are so many things I could say but none of the words would live up to the absolute wonderful chaos that is my life. I'm a mother. A therapist, wife, and daughter. I'm a reader and a writer.

I'm a woman who has never forgotten how often her twelve-year-old self dreamed of being an author. I've always said writing is my dream and mental health is my passion. I am motivated and blessed enough to peruse both while loving my family with my whole heart and soul.

The hard days are tough. The lows are pretty deep. And the highs... they are what I live for. Being everything that I am has come with challenges but wow are they beautiful ones.

The pages you'll read show emotion and despair because I am not only the roles I fill for others. I was a kid who felt loss and internal pain. That part of me is still in there begging to be seen and heard... so this is me... my trauma dump in dramatic form. My FMC's live horrible lives, and while their experiences are far beyond mine, their feelings are often my own.

I struggle and I cry. I feel worthless and sometimes like I'm fighting every day just to be enough. Their stories are mine in a way. Please read with empathy as trauma responses are different for everyone.

My stories and yours are valid and worth being heard. Don't ever lose sight of the battles you've overcome.

And take care of yourself, please.
With appreciation and empathy,
Y.V. Larson

www.ingramcontent.com/pod-product-compliance
Lightning Source LLC
Chambersburg PA
CBHW071146260626
47162CB00003B/940